No Ordinary Man

S. Carman Knight

No Ordinary Man

Copyright©2014 Susan Keenan

This book is a work of fiction. Names, characters, places, and incidents are either a product of the author's imagination or are used fictitiously. Any resemblance to events, business establishments, locales, or actual persons, living or dead is coincidental.

No part of this book may be reproduced without permission of the author.

The support of the author's rights is appreciated.

Dear Reader,

No Ordinary Man is a contemporary romance with suspense and intrigue. I hope you enjoy reading it as much as I enjoyed writing it. I would love to hear from you. You can contact me at scknight@rochester.rr.com. You can find me at http://www.scarmanknight.com and Facebook where you will also see information about upcoming releases.

I wish you all the best.
S. Carman Knight

Acknowledgements

A special thanks to my dear friend Leslie. I thank her for her editing expertise, but above all, I thank her for her support.

CHAPTER ONE

Hannah Swift brushed a kernel of Styrofoam from the cool limestone surface of the sculpture. Empty eyes stared back at her, the eyes of a man from another time.

Only he wasn't.

The sculpture cradled in the packing crate was not the real Blochet.

Hannah stepped aside so that the curator of Toronto's Royal Victoria Museum could remove the life-sized head from its crate.

"Breathtaking, isn't he," said Dr. Edgar Dewald.

"Breathtaking," Hannah said and tried to convince herself she was mistaken about the Blochet, the common name for *L'homme Ordinaire*. The owner herself, Simona Poole Kenyon, had supervised the delicate packing process, and from the moment the crates were closed, they had become Hannah's responsibility.

Pieces of the greenish packing material clung to Dr. Dewald's delicate hands as he reached for the ancient Egyptian head. From nearby Hannah observed the curator carefully for any cues, however slight, that the sculpture now in his temporary care was not authentic. Dewald raised the Blochet gently from the bed of airy plastic that surrounded it and then, halfway to its temporary home, he paused and, turning it carefully in the bright overhead light, gazed into the face of the most interesting piece of early Egyptian sculpture to grace the Royal Victoria Museum's latest exhibit.

"Magnificent," he said and moments later set the Blochet on the base that would be its resting place for the next three months. With no indication that the sculpture was anything other than exactly what it was purported to be, he began the delicate process of securing a padded ring that would hold it firmly in place.

From behind the narrow chrome obelisk where the head now rested, Hannah forced herself to take another breath. Then she stepped forward until she was inches from the priceless work. The simple bronze placard riveted to the obelisk proclaimed the sculpture's academic name in both of Canada's official languages, *L'homme Ordinaire* – *The Common Man*. But there was nothing common about this Egyptian man.

Dewald lowered the heavy Plexiglas covering over the sculpture, matching the contact points for the alarm. "There," Dewald said for himself, then turned to Hannah, his smile filled with pride. "Not a scratch on him. You be certain to let Simona know *L'homme* is safe and secure."

"I'll let her know," Hannah said, but it was not Simona Poole Kenyon who needed reassurance. It was her son, Jesher Kenyon. Jesher had opposed the idea of his mother's parting with any piece of the family art collection for any reason, even one so philanthropic as a temporary exhibit of Egyptian art from the Old Kingdom.

"And be sure to tell Simona," Dewald was saying, "that the Victoria Museum is eternally grateful, I am eternally grateful." He spread his hands expansively. "A reserve head," he said and shook his own slowly in awe. "Imagine that. A sculpture whose purpose remains as mysterious as its smile. Having *L'homme Ordinaire* as part of our early dynastic exhibit is a coup for the Vic," he stepped back to admire the sculpture, "and an unprecedented opportunity for the public to view such a treasure."

Next to Hannah, her brother Turner shifted his stance in coiled impatience. Turner was a restless man whose once unstoppable smile now rarely showed itself. Taller than Hannah by half a foot, he bore the genetic echo of the Swift family – full lips, curling black hair and pale blue eyes. Eyes that at the moment were trained on his sister.

"If you'll follow me," Dewald was saying, "I'll show you where the next piece is to be placed."

Without comment her brother took the handle of the hand truck and rolled it over the terrazzo floors just behind Edgar Dewald.

Four years ago Turner had become chief of security for the AmRaq Oil Company in the Middle East. The job took advantage of his military training and offered him the high stakes adventure that was missing from his civilian life. But three years in, there was a problem, the only solution for which appeared to be American cash and plenty of it. Turner had never volunteered specifics and Hannah had never asked, but she had sent him her entire savings and when that wasn't enough, she had left her job as assistant curator at the Phipps Gallery for a more lucrative position as personal assistant to the eccentric Simona Poole Kenyon.

Now Turner was back in New York, picking up work where he could find it. Driving her to Toronto had been Hannah's idea. She was to accompany the museum couriers' van to assure the safe arrival of the artifacts, and she didn't relish the idea of making the long trek alone. Having Turner along would ease the monotony, her brother could earn a little cash, and just maybe if he played his cards right, he could wrangle a job out of it running security for Jesher's firm.

"You coming, Ms. Swift?" Dewald asked.

Hannah looked away from her brother to the

fragile man beside him. "In a moment."

The curator smiled. "I understand. No matter how many times I view a work of this caliber, it never fails to mesmerize me. Take your time. We'll just be here."

Hannah stepped in front of the sculpture. The almond shaped eyes were perfectly symmetrical and lightly ridged suggesting thick Kohl liner, the long narrow eyebrows were flawlessly formed. A broad nose rose slowly from the stone's surface, and below that, heavy lips, their corners raised in an enigmatic smile. A classic image of an Egyptian male, rendered in the stylized fashion of the Fourth Dynasty.

It was perfect.

It was the real Blochet.

It had to be.

How could it be anything else?

Hannah had been mistaken even to entertain the notion that this sculpture, whose maker had infused such life force into a lifeless chunk of stone, could be anything but the same piece that had topped the slender column in the private rooms at Simona's estate.

Hannah moved slowly, circling the obelisk and the sculpture it supported. Deep incising marks that began at the forehead roughed in a hairline before finally ending at the base of the skull. Traces of red and black paint, all but invisible in the glow of an ordinary incandescent bulb, showed clearly in the full spectrum museum lighting. Then she stepped forward for a better look.

And felt her heart level a single thud.
This was not the Blochet Head.

In the next room Hannah could hear Edgar Dewald's slow, rhythmical tones as he detailed a canopic jar for Turner who didn't even pretend to care. She had to let someone know that the reserve head now in residence at Toronto's Royal Victoria Museum was not the one owned by Simona Poole Kenyon.

And she had to do it right away.

Telling Dr. Dewald was out of the question. It would be an item of ethical embarrassment to point up so weighty a piece as an imposter. Dr. Dewald was, after all, the curator of one of the finest museums in North America. Besides, he would undoubtedly call into question her limited knowledge of Egyptian sculpture from the Old Kingdom and no doubt remind her that she was only Simona's personal assistant.

Just as easily, Hannah rejected telling Simona. Simona Poole Kenyon was, put simply, emotionally undependable. From the continuum of potential responses to such horrible news, Hannah had no way to predict where this woman's reaction would lie. And a loose cannon she did not need.

That left Jesher.

Hannah closed her eyes. Jesher had insisted she accompany his mother's precious artifacts to the Vic to assure their safety and proper handling. Now she had to let him know that one of his mother's irreplaceable Egyptian treasures had, in fact, been replaced. A sickening feeling crept over her. Hannah shook it off and reached for her cell phone.

Jesher answered on the second ring. His husky voice was quiet and even, momentarily distracting Hannah with its soothing cadence just as it always did.

"There's a bit of a situation here at the Vic," she said and imagined the stark features of his face tightening down.

"What kind of situation?" he asked.

Hannah glanced into the next room. Dewald was bent over the final crate, but Turner was staring past the older man directly at his sister. She walked farther away from the curator and her brother. "The Blochet doesn't look right," was all she said. Then she closed her eyes and waited.

Her simple statement met dead air.

"How so?" he said finally. His terse choice of phrase belied the sensuality his tone projected.

It was a question Hannah had known would come, just as she imagined other, more probing questions would follow. "The paint is wrong. Something else, too, I think. Something about the mouth." She knew her answer wasn't good enough for a man like Jesher. Because Jesher Kenyon was bathed in practicality.

At last unable to stand his calculated silence she added, "I thought you should know right away."

"I assume you haven't told anyone else."

Hannah's shoes made small clicking noises against the terrazzo floors as she walked back to the obelisk and the stone head it supported. "No," she said. "No one."

"Good. Keep it that way."

"Don't you think Dr. Dewald should –?"

"No one. Is that clear?" Jesher's words cut across hers as he underscored his command.

Hannah nodded. "Yes."

"When are you leaving?"

"Dr. Dewald is securing the last item now, the polished stone model. If the rain lets up we should be back well before midnight."

"Come to my office as soon as you get back."

The phone went dead in Hannah's hand. She dropped it into her purse and went to join her brother and Edgar Dewald.

Three and a half hours later, Hannah walked through the doors of Jesher's office. Kenyon International was a first generation enterprise dedicated to locating fine and rare art for anyone willing to pay for the beauty and prestige such treasures imparted. Hannah had met face to face with Jesher only a handful of times. Theirs was an acquaintance sustained instead by phone calls and voice mails. What little she knew of the man had been culled from casual conversations with Simona, frequently over afternoon tea.

Hannah knew that Jesher was on the late side of thirty, born to Simona when she had all but given up having children. Hannah knew that he was the only child of Simona and Alistair Kenyon, though there was a half-sister Lily that lived not far away. She also knew that he had shunned his mother's wealth and in less than ten years had taken his start-up company and turned it into a highly profitable business of international prestige.

And while Simona was rightfully proud of her son's accomplishments, she disapproved of the manner in which he had realized his success. She had taught Jesher much of what he knew about art in hopes of igniting in him a lasting appreciation for what the better side of man could produce. Instead, Jesher had taken that knowledge and used it to turn a handsome profit and Hannah sensed that Jesher's mantle of practicality was Alistair's doing.

What more Hannah knew of Jesher was folkloric. He was reputed to like Bombay Sapphire gin, unfettered affairs of short duration with beautiful women, and the unaccompanied keyboard works of J.S. Bach, although not necessarily in that order. And although he enjoyed spending the money he had earned, she sensed that with him it was more about the hunt than the meal.

There were also stories of questionable overseas business dealings, one involving a member of Phoenix, a multinational coalition of eastern Mediterranean mobsters. And more recently there had been rumors that his brief engagement to Savatheda Christiana was over. This last tidbit was no surprise to the gossip columnists. What had been a surprise was that there was an engagement at all.

Hannah dropped her linen jacket to one of the chairs facing Jesher's desk and looked at him straight on. He was a tall man, lean and fit, with hair the color of bitter chocolate and an angular face that translated his mother's delicate beauty into rugged masculinity. He was dressed solidly in black – sleek ribbed sweater and easy slacks, a look which underscored the solemnity his face projected. Even as she watched, he allowed his green eyes to measure her coolly.

"I've been thinking about it all the way back," Hannah said. "I should have said something to Dr. Dewald." She caught up a strand of her hair that had worked free from its French braid and tucked it behind her ear. "His reputation could be on the line."

"No," Jesher said. He removed his frameless glasses, folded the gold earpieces in on themselves and set them on his desk. "You did the right thing. You should never air doubts of authenticity if you can't back them up."

He stood and walked to the front of his desk. Jesher studied Hannah with the same detached professionalism he used to evaluate a work of art. The interest her face held, he decided as his eyes settled on it, came from the careful contrasts nature had bestowed. The elegant structure of her cheeks was offset by soft, full lips, while pale eyes juxtaposed the warm tones of her honey skin and curling black hair. All in all a disarmingly attractive woman, though not his type at all. Too small, too unsophisticated, and entirely too serious. "So tell me," he went on, "how certain are you that the real Blochet is not at the Vic?" He picked up his glasses momentarily before once

10

again setting them aside.

"Simona has had it in her studio recently. There's something about the mouth she likes. She's been working on a study." Hannah closed her eyes and tried to capture the differences between the Blochet she had seen in the studio and the one at the Vic. Even as she attempted to envision the sculptures, she could feel Jesher scrutinizing every detail of her face, as if she herself were a forgery. She opened her eyes and found him just as she had suspected, examining her like a butterfly pinned to cotton batting. She met his eyes in a challenge. "I'm almost one hundred percent sure," she told him.

"Not good enough," Jesher said and rubbed absently at the bridge of his nose where his glasses had left small, dark indentations. "I need to see it for myself."

"Before you call the police?"

Behind him, his computer beeped. Jesher leaned across his desk and silenced it with a keystroke. Beneath the sleek sweater, deeply corded muscles contracted and relaxed as they slid over bone, hinting at a controlled power that had no business in the art world. "Before I do anything," he said, turning back.

"But the Blochet and whoever took it could be anywhere by then."

"Or nowhere."

Hannah looked up at the man leaning casually against the polished mahogany desk, knowing there was nothing casual about anything he did. Or said. But she had no intention of asking him what he meant. "Then why am I here?" she said instead. "I thought you wanted me to talk to the police, tell them what I know."

Without responding, Jesher straightened away from the desk and walked back to his chair. Then he lowered his gaze to the computer screen, his forehead furrowing slightly at what he saw. Eventually he looked away from his work to the small woman seated before him. "The police don't know the first thing about locating art of this caliber," he said. "They'll spread a broad net and hope for the best. Meanwhile the Blochet will slip through it and likely be lost forever. Once art is forced underground, it attracts a different class of buyers, people who set their own rules."

Hannah reached for her blazer where it lay beside her and drew it about her shoulders to ward off a shiver. Like his mother, Jesher seemed to prefer indoor temperatures hovering at the unbearably cold. "But this is a criminal matter," she insisted. "Surely the police should be informed."

There was another period of artful silence in which Jesher's gaze met Hannah's with the predatory intensity of a feral challenge. "This isn't your call, Hannah," he said finally, his voice barely above a whisper. Then he stood and walked to the bank of windows where he looked down on the rain-swollen waters of the Genesee River. "You're here," he added after a time, "because I want you to detail the transport of my mother's pieces to the Vic. Tell me everything from the time they were crated until the time you phoned me. I want to know who helped you with the transport. I want to know who drove the van, who loaded and unloaded the crates. I want to know where and when you stopped during transport, if the crates left your sight and for how long. I want to know who had coffee and how they took it." He paused to let the words sink in. "Everything."

For the next half hour Hannah recounted each detail and Jesher listened without interruption, never once turning from his view of a nighttime river tormented by the rains of spring. When she finished, he returned to his desk. "I need to see the Blochet for myself. The least conspicuous way to manage that is at the patrons' gala this Saturday evening. I want you there with me," he told her.

Hannah Swift hadn't just fallen off the turnip truck. Jesher was not issuing an invitation for her to be his guest; he was issuing an order. And despite the fact that he was, she supposed, ultimately her employer, she didn't much like being ordered about. She looked him squarely in his impossibly green eyes and took a turn at his game, allowing the silence to grow between them until it begged to be broken.

Moments passed and then slow smile inched its way across Jesher's face, smoothing out the harsh lines it found there.

Hannah had parted her lips to speak when she caught herself. Instead, she narrowed her eyes. She knew his smile was meant to take the edge off the tension, just enough to lure her into a response.

Jesher's smile deepened. At last he lofted one of his thick straight eyebrows. "You'll come as my guest, of course," he said quietly. Then he picked up his glasses, snapped them into a case and stuffed them into his pocket. "Get your things, I'll take you home."

"Why do you want me at the gala," she asked and slipped into her jacket. I've told you everything I know."

"Mother will be there," he returned. "And she is very fond of you. If anyone can distract her, you can. And if the Blochet's the fake you claim, she'll need distracting."

As Hannah walked to the door, she felt Jesher's fingers lightly against the small of her back in an oddly proprietary gesture. "Can't you talk her out of coming? It would be a lot easier than trying to run interference."

"Not likely. Things usually go Mother's way. She sees to it. She is very single-minded."

"A family trait?" Hannah said before she could stop herself.

A light smile played on Jesher's lips but he refused the bait. "If she thinks the sculpture isn't hers," he said instead, "the whole gala could end in a blaze of glory. You need to see that doesn't happen. But right now you need to report back to Mother. I'll drive you home to Pinehurst tonight and tomorrow, before she has a chance to ask for specifics, you tell her how smoothly

But Hannah was shaking her head. "I can't do that. How can I face Simona and pretend that everything is fine when it isn't?"

"You'll just have to act."

Hannah rolled her eyes.

"You've done a fine job of it so far."

Something in his tone sent a warning shiver across Hannah's shoulders "What are you implying?" she asked him. "Do you think that I don't really care that the Blochet has been taken?"

When he didn't immediately respond Hannah stopped walking and turned to face him. Despite his size, Jesher was agile. He stopped short, barely leaving air between them. Then he held his place, letting himself loom over her tiny frame.

"I never said you didn't care." His voice was soft, almost sensuous.

"Then what?" she asked.

"I put you in charge of the Blochet from the time the museum couriers arrived until Dewald put it on the obelisk and fired up the alarm."

Hannah couldn't believe what he was saying. She felt a cold chill run the length of her spine. "And you think I am somehow involved in this?"

She was met with another one of Jesher's interminable silences. She held her ground, the anger she felt neatly placed on her tight lips. And she waited for his reply.

"I intend to find out," he said, finally and pushed

the elevator call button.

CHAPTER TWO

Hannah stood at the entrance to the Royal Victoria Museum while patrons filtered through the massive bronze doors.

"Sorry to keep you waiting, dear," Simona said and released the folds of her skirt from her slender hand. Layers of shimmering red silk swirled about her ankles. "That was Malcolm Hewett, a dear friend. Remind me to introduce you later," she smiled broadly. "He's quite the catch."

A brisk gust of April wind shivered Hannah's bare shoulders. "I appreciate the gesture, Simona, but I'm not really looking."

"Don't be silly," Simona said and patted Hannah's hand. "Of course you are. Everyone's looking, even when they shouldn't be. Trust me on that one. I was married to Alistair through too many of his cheesy affairs." She tossed her head in a well-practiced gesture and as Hannah watched, her silky pageboy, today rinsed with Ebony Magic, settled into place. "Besides, a little healthy competition might be just the ticket for that son of mine."

Hannah furrowed her brow.

"I have no doubt," Simona went on, "that Jesher was nosing down some Picasso sketch or other this afternoon when he should have been driving up here with you. After all, he is your escort this evening." She pursed her lips.

Earlier in the day Jesher had left Hannah a voice

mail saying that he had ordered a car for her and his mother and that he would join them at the gala. He had offered no apology or explanation, not that Hannah expected either. After all, he had turned her concern over the Blochet's authenticity upside down, shaken out an accusation and set it squarely in her lap.

"With my son," Simona went on, "business takes precedence over anything else, which, if you ask me, encouraged Savatheda's wandering ways. Not that I cared much for her, you understand."

Hannah understood quite well; Simona had made no bones about her feelings toward the young woman whose name had been romantically linked to the Brazilian entrepreneur Paulo Jobim even while she wore Jesher's diamond. When news of Savatheda's infidelity had found its way to the *Living* section of the **Rochester Chronicle** and then **The New York Sun Post**, Jesher had quietly ended the engagement. But that had been almost a year ago and since that time Jesher had seemed to have eyes only for his work.

"I think," Hannah said, "that you may have misunderstood the intent of Jesher's invitation. I am here because he thought you might enjoy some company this evening and because he knew I would be interested in seeing the exhibit in its entirety. Nothing more." She mentally winced at the lie, however white, and tried to focus on the larger truth, the need to avert the disaster that would certainly follow if Simona saw the Blochet. Or, rather, if she didn't see it.

Simona lifted one of her flawlessly arched eyebrows. "And that, I suppose, is why you're wearing such a delicious gown for the occasion? To be seen with me?"

Hannah felt her cheeks darken. The dress she had chosen was a glittery, two-piece affair that had nothing to do with her daily fare of natural fibers and earth tones. The gown's figure hugging, black sequined top left bare her shoulders and much of her back, and skimmed the waist of the skirt formed with layers of shimmering black taffeta that billowed to her ankles. Hannah shivered again. "Can we go in?" was her only response.

Inside the museum, more than five hundred people were already celebrating *Voices From The Past*, the most extensive exhibit of early dynastic Egyptian art and artifacts ever assembled in North America. Strategically placed stelae teased onlookers with the promise of glimpses into North African life four thousand years before. Scarlet banners, hung from the domed foyer ceiling, lent an air of festivity to the staid, old building. And replicas of royal chariots flanked the broad staircase and pointed the way to the exhibit beyond. While a few people had wandered upstairs, most were enjoying champagne while awaiting the official greeting from the head curator of the Royal Victoria Museum, Dr. Edgar Dewald.

"Eddie's done a fine job of it," Simona said when she had looked the foyer over. "I should find him and let him know." She scanned the noisy crowd, but not immediately seeing her friend, lightly shrugged off the notion. "Later, then. He's sure to be about all evening." She retrieved the hem of her gown with one hand while she nudged Hannah forward slightly with the other. "Shall we go?"

Hannah's face formed an unspoken question.

"To the exhibit, dear. That is why we came, after all."

Counting on deep crowds to separate Simona from the Blochet, Hannah had devised no other diversion. But at the moment those crowds were still in the foyer sipping champagne, seeing and being seen by collectors and aficionados of Egyptian art from both the U.S. and Canada. If she and Simona went upstairs now only Plexiglas would separate Simona from a very, very good copy of the Blochet Head. "Shouldn't we wait?" Hannah suggested.

Mild impatience worked its way across Simona's high forehead. "For what? Edgar's dreary speech? I rather think not. He's a nice man, and knowledgeable in his own field – Sumerian statuary – but frankly he doesn't know a hill of beans about Fourth Dynasty Egyptian art." With her hand she urged Hannah forward. "Besides, it will be a generic welcome. You know the kind. 'This exhibit is not the work of one man but a collaborative effort – '" She completed the thought with an elegant flourish of her hand.

Hannah tried again. "I meant Jesher." She paused to scan the crowd for the man. Surely he had a plan to keep his mother from the Blochet. "It would be nice to see the exhibit with him."

Simona slowly turned to Hannah, her handsome face posed in typical Kenyon inscrutability. "So," she said eventually and lifted her chin slightly, "I thought as much." With her cool, green eyes she took Hannah on. "You are interested in him after all, despite your careless attitude toward him. You wait then, you really should." She allowed a brief smile and started forward again. "I'm going on ahead of the crowds so I can enjoy the exhibit in relative peace."

Options and time were fast abandoning Hannah. Snagging two crystal flutes from a passing waiter, she plunked one in the older woman's hand. "We should celebrate the opening," she said. "Champagne?"

Simona looked briefly at the glass before returning her gaze to Hannah. "I really shouldn't," she said. "Jesher says I – "

"Well, Jesher isn't here, now is he?" Hannah returned and silently cursed the man's absence.

"I don't suppose one glass would hurt, just to toast," she said and raised hers. "After all, this is the first time any of the Poole collection has been publicly viewed."

Hannah nodded absently. Her eyes were on the crowd, searching out Jesher. Her mind was on the task at hand, preventing Simona from getting more than a passing glance at her beloved limestone head.

"To Pierre," Simona said and lightly touched her flute to Hannah's.

Hannah blinked. "Pierre?"

"Blochet. Pierre Blochet was the archaeologist who discovered *L'homme Ordinaire* and four other reserve heads buried beside the tombs of the royal household. What makes *L'homme Ordinaire* so special is that it was the only head believed to be that of a common man. Truly magnificent, my Blochet," Simona said, "and unique in all the world." She paused and upended her glass. "The toast was an excellent idea. Now, I am anxious to see the exhibit."

Even as Hannah watched, Simona deposited her flute on the tray of a passing waiter and started for the second floor of the Royal Victoria Museum. Hannah reached for two more glasses and caught up with her at the foot of the staircase. She held out a flute to Simona. "I would like to toast Dr. Dewald. He has done an exceptional job with this exhibit."

Simona took the flute from Hannah and raised it high. "Well, just one more. After all, I do love a bit of the bubbly," she said and took a swallow. "To Eddie."

A long arm reached over Simona's head and plucked the glass from her fingers.

"You're a killjoy," Simona said without glancing around.

"You're flushed," Jesher returned and handed off the glass.

Hannah turned toward the husky voice behind her. Like everyone attending the gala tonight, Jesher had donned formal attire. But unlike many, he wore his traditional tuxedo with as much ease as he had worn his sweater and casual trousers the night before.

"You're here," Hannah breathed and felt herself relax a bit. "I was beginning to think you weren't going to make it."

Jesher lowered his chin slightly and took in the woman by his mother's side. But tonight his eyes weren't devouring Hannah like an entomological specimen; tonight he was sipping her like a rare wine. Because tonight this woman looked nothing like the functionally streamlined person who kept his mother's daily calendar – and life – in perfect order.

Jesher allowed his eyes to meander from the loose cluster of black curls held from Hannah's face by no more than a pin or two, to his mother's black pearl choker at her throat. There he paused to enjoy the blush of color that rose to her cheeks, knowing that he had put it there. Then his eyes wandered to the shimmery black bandeau and the soft swell of breasts that rose and fell with each breath she took. He felt himself stir and forced his eyes away from her.

It occurred briefly to Jesher that Hannah knew nothing of the heady response she evoked in him, dressed as she was with so much of her delicious, tawny skin exposed. Just as easily, he tossed aside the notion. Experience reminded him that women of her merit knew the effect they had on men. And they used it like a home field advantage.

Eventually Jesher returned his attention to his mother. "Would you like to see the exhibit, Mother?" he said and kissed her cheek.

"That would be lovely," Simona returned.

"You lead the way, then," Jesher said and urged her forward with a tilt of his head. Then he took Hannah's elbow, holding her back until his mother had sifted into the crowd. "Nice job," he whispered into her hair. "I leave Mother in your care and you get her drunk."

"I've done nothing of the sort," came Hannah's sharp return. "You told me to keep her away from the Blochet and I was doing the best I could under extenuating circumstances."

"Extenuating circumstances? You knew Mother and the Blochet both would be here."

Hannah's irritation rose at his apparent need to press the obvious. "But I expected you to be here as well," she went on and willed down the blood that had risen sharply to her cheeks.

"And here I am," Jesher returned, his husky tone oddly soothing to Hannah despite her exasperation.

"Besides, she only had one glass," she added by way of her own defense.

"She shouldn't have had any."

"Look, Jesher," Hannah said and tried to wriggle free from the hold he had on her elbow, "she's an adult, she knows her limits. And anyway it was one glass of champagne. One lousy glass."

"She can't have anything with alcohol in it," he said. "Not even hard sauce. She has a bad reaction." Jesher kept firm his hold on Hannah's arm, noting with less practiced detachment than pleased him, that beneath the pad of his thumb, her skin was smooth and soft. And if he moved his hand slightly, he could feel the steady cadence of her pulse on the satin flesh just inside her elbow.

"She looks fine to me," Hannah was saying. "A little glittery, maybe, but she seemed to enjoy the wine."

"It makes her tense," Jesher replied. "That's her word for it. The doctors call it alcohol induced situational anxiety." He allowed his fingers to flex and shift against the delicate skin they warmed.

"Then why," Hannah said over her shoulder, "are we heading to the exhibit? Because seeing what is meant to pass for the Blochet won't do much to relieve her tension."

"It seems like the logical thing to do," Jesher returned and steered her through an opening in the crowd.

"You'll have to help me out here, Jesher, because I'm having trouble following your logic."

"Damage control," was all he said.

Hannah wasn't certain what he meant and she never had the opportunity to ask. Just ahead of them, Simona waited at the foot of the grand staircase with Malcolm Hewett anchored firmly at her side.

"Look who's latched onto Mother," Jesher said and tugged Hannah to a halt. "I wonder what he wants." The evening was turning out far worse than he had anticipated. He felt the familiar throbbing at his temples, reached for his glasses and slipped the delicate gold wires over his ears. Then he blinked deeply and tried to adjust to the vague distortion the glasses brought.

"I think Simona has a little matchmaking in mind," Hannah told him.

"She's going to fix up Hewett?"

"That's what she said," Hannah replied.

"With whom?"

Hannah turned to face Jesher. Shimmering lengths of black taffeta whispered their reply to her movement. "Why me, of course." She smiled up at him with what she hoped was irritating sweetness.

Jesher's eyes narrowed almost imperceptibly as he contemplated the potential fallout from such a union. "A word of friendly advice," he said finally. "Don't get yourself tangled with the likes of Malcolm Hewett. He's bad news."

"Your mother doesn't seem to think so."

The muscles in Jesher's jaws knotted briefly. "Mother only knows him through his collection of flatwork."

"Is it decent, this flatwork of his?"

"I've seen better," Jesher said.

Hannah felt the intensity of his gaze and shifted her stance away from him as if doing so would offer her protection. "So tell me about the Malcolm Hewett you know."

"Hewett did some work for me a while back," he said. Then he carefully removed his glasses, and with a cloth from his breast pocket cleaned a speck of dust from one of the lenses.

Getting Jesher Kenyon to talk in anything other than the briefest of sentences was like trying to hoe a garden with a spoon. "But no more?" she pressed when it appeared he had no intention of pursuing the conversation further.

Jesher shook his head. "While negotiating for several pieces of statuary, Hewett managed to unilaterally piss off the Turkish government. I tried to salvage what I could of the deal. A colossal waste of everyone's time." He paused and put his glasses on again. "In the eyes of the Turkish government, Hewett was an envoy from Kenyon International and therefore only doing my bidding. The man singlehandedly destroyed the relationship I had been nurturing for the last five years."

"So you handed him his Samsonite and sent him off to reign terror on another firm."

"Hewett doesn't actually work for anybody but himself, a fact I wish I had known before I took him on." Jesher allowed himself to linger for a moment over the details of Hannah's face. Sweeping black lashes fringed eyes of delicate opalescent blue. A man less careful than he was could lose himself in such pale pools of color. "Consider yourself warned, Hannah Swift," he added almost as an afterthought. "He's a bad actor. Worse, he's a womanizer."

That said, Jesher took Hannah's forearm, brought her around to his side and stepped up to his mother and Malcolm.

"Jesher, Hannah. Look who I found," Simona said.

She slipped her arm through Malcolm's and held him firmly in place.

Beside her Malcolm beamed. "Good to see you, man," he said and held out his hand to Jesher who shook it more out of good breeding than good friendship.

Malcolm Hewett was tall and lean with a uniformly handsome face whose even features added little character. His chestnut hair was combed straight back from his forehead in a style meant to mimic Jesher's, and his rich tan told tales of perfect Caribbean beaches.

Simona adjusted her red silk stole. "Let me introduce you, Malcolm," she said. Her smile was a bit brittle and Hannah noticed that she appeared to be blinking more frequently than usual. "This is my personal assistant, Hannah Swift. Hannah," she reached for Hannah's hand, "Malcolm Hewett," and placed it squarely in Malcolm's grasp.

"A pleasure," Hannah said. "Jesher was just telling me what a fine collection of flatwork you have."

"Really?" Malcolm glanced just past Hannah to Jesher who smiled coolly. "If you're interested, I would be more than happy to give you a tour some evening. Perhaps over dinner?"

"I'd like that," Hannah said. Next to her, Jesher shifted his stance bringing him so close she could feel the heat his body radiated.

"Are we ready, then?" Simona asked. "Eddie's about to speak and soon everyone will be clamoring up these stairs." She turned to Jesher. "You know how I hate crowds, dear."

Malcolm still held Hannah's hand. "Shall we?"

Hannah offered up one helpless look in Jesher's direction before she gathered her taffeta skirts and followed Malcolm up the staircase.

Voices From The Past occupied the two upper floors of the Royal Victoria Museum and included pieces from twenty-two public facilities around the world as well as a dozen private collections. Despite Hannah's extensive exposure to early Egyptian art, she couldn't help but be impressed. The Phipps Gallery where she had worked for four years was a small facility whose most aggressive attempt to play in the major leagues was landing a one-month stop on a tour of Maxfield Parrish's original canvases and drawings. But this exhibit was, in itself, a work of art.

Hannah paused at a portrait statue of Mycerinus and his queen, an awe-inspiring sculpture in slate that reflected both power and affection.

Malcolm drew close to her side. "I wish I knew more about Egyptian work from this period," he said. "I understand from Simona that you've got a strong background in the ancients." He turned slightly into her. "So tell me, what makes this statue so special, besides its obvious beauty?"

Hannah shared what she knew of that piece and the others they encountered as they wandered from display to display. It was easy to be with him, Hannah decided. The intensity so deeply embedded in Jesher was peacefully absent in Malcolm Hewett. Malcolm drew her easily into conversation using the exhibits before them as quiet steppingstones into her personal life. Before she realized it, she had told him intimate insignificances from her childhood, which included her first kiss with Bobby Weyland and the ride she sneaked in her next-door neighbor's car.

An hour into the exhibit, Hannah remembered why she was at the opening Gala. Just past the monumental seated statue of Hemiunu stood a solitary obelisk, and on it the reserve head of *L'homme Ordinaire*. In the distance Jesher's raspy tones came to her as he chatted with his mother about a recently acquired client.

Simona's frequent responses to her son came in a series of breathy laughs. Despite the small amount of champagne Simona had drunk, it seemed apparent that Jesher's assessment of his mother's edgy physical state had been accurate. It remained to see how her alcohol-induced anxiety would play out when she realized the fabulous reserve head on display was not hers.

"There it is," Malcolm said and nodded in the direction of the Blochet. "I'm glad Simona changed her mind and loaned it to the Vic. She turned down Dr. Dewald when he first approached her, you know."

"Jesher didn't think it was a good idea either."

"We make a good team, you and I." Malcolm's voice was silky, intimate.

Hannah drew to a halt. "What do you mean?"

"I urged Simona to rethink Dewald's request. I told her the art world shouldn't be deprived of a piece as magnificent as the Blochet. But in the end I don't think she would have recanted if you hadn't accompanied her pieces here."

"I was happy to do it. I knew Jesher had concerns about the safety of his mother's collection." Hannah drew in a long breath, satisfied that she had skirted the conversation with Jesher in which he had made the trip incumbent on the retention of her employment.

"Jesher's concerns were monetary," Malcolm returned. "The Blochet is beyond dollar value. Insurance could never pay its full worth and he knows it."

"It's Simona's statue," Hannah said.

Malcolm blinked slowly. "For now. But by terms of his grandfather's will, the Blochet and its companion pieces will someday be his. They must be passed on, follow bloodlines. They can never be – you'll excuse the expression – disposed of. So you see, Jesher was only protecting his interests. For me," he continued, "it's different. Art is my life. For Jesher, I'm afraid it is only a commodity."

Hannah ran the tip of her tongue over her lips. Jesher had never denied his reputation for ruthless business dealings. Maybe he saw no need to defend himself. Or maybe he simply didn't care what others thought of him. It was, at any rate, fodder for later ruminations. At the moment there was the matter of Simona and the statue.

Hannah spotted Jesher meandering through the last of the stelae. Simona, on the other hand was rapidly bearing down on her beloved artifact, the skirt of her red gown strewn behind her like a speedboat wake. "Could you excuse me for a minute?" Hannah said.

Malcolm nodded amiably and strolled through the immense arch and into the adjoining room.

Four steps brought Hannah to Jesher's side. "What's the plan?" she said and nodded once over her shoulder.

Jesher carefully removed his glasses and rubbed the bridge of his nose.

Irritation at his silence eventually displaced Hannah's control. "Jesher? As we speak your mother – your tense mother – is about to view the Blochet, or rather what should be the Blochet. So, I ask you again. What's the plan?" She turned just enough to see Simona scoop up Malcolm who stood transfixed at the polished stone phallus meant to symbolize the life force of Egypt.

"The plan was your territory, remember?" Jesher replied easily.

Hannah ignored the throaty timber of his voice and focused on his message. "My territory?" she returned. "No way. You're not pinning this one on me." She shook her head, releasing a soft citrusy scent into the air.

Beside her Jesher inhaled deeply. "That's why you're here. You do remember that I wanted you to distract Mother."

"How can I distract her when you've led her right to ground zero?"

Jesher shrugged easily. "But if I were you," he added, "I'd think of something." He glanced over Hannah's head. "And soon."

It wasn't just his calm, even tones that irritated Hannah so. It was his apparent willingness to watch a disaster unfold, all the while pinning the wretched affair neatly on her bare shoulders. Unless, of course she was mistaken about the authenticity of the reserve head now perched atop the obelisk.

Slowly she turned back to Jesher and narrowed her eyes. "You've already been up here, haven't you?" She didn't even try to keep the accusatory tone from her words. "You came up here and saw the Blochet before you found your mother and me downstairs. That's why you were late." She barely stopped for breath. "I was wrong about the sculpture, wasn't I? It's authentic and that's why you aren't trying to stop your mother."

"You weren't wrong," Jesher said quietly. He couldn't help but notice how the vein at the base of her throat throbbed with her apparent agitation.

Hannah closed her eyes and let the terrible words become reality. "The Blochet's a fake?"

"As the proverbial three dollar bill."

"Then why," she said, unable to rein in her anger, "are you standing here?"

Jesher frowned. "Where should I stand?"

"A place to start might be between your mother

and that fake in the next room," she returned.

Jesher didn't respond right away. Instead he stood poised near the stelae, watching as Simona walked straight to the obelisk and the prize it held. Then he shrugged and turned his attention to a case of stone Shabti figures.

"Jesher?" Hannah said. "For the love of heaven, do something."

An odd, strangled sound emanated from the next room.

"Too late," he replied without looking up.

CHAPTER THREE

Hannah let the honey-scented Riesling play across her tongue. The wine was a perfect foil for the tidbit of Gorgonzola she had just tasted. Her host had chosen well. But then everything that Malcolm orchestrated, it seemed, was perfectly accomplished. She glanced around the solarium where she waited, while in another room Malcolm selected the wines to be served with dinner.

French windows enclosed the room on three sides, leaving only the wall shared with the living room on which to display some of the more capricious pieces from Malcolm's flatwork collection. Hannah took another sip of wine and contemplated his decision to partner a Manet with a Max Ernst.

"The Ernst is a favorite of mine," Malcolm said.

Hannah turned to see him standing in the broad, arched opening that led back to the more formal part of the house.

"Though I can't tell you why," he went on.

"It's unusual," she said.

"It's ridiculous," he returned, "but then much of Surrealism is not meant to be taken seriously, is it? The Impressionists are certainly prettier, if that's the most that can be said for them." He moved into the room and freshened her goblet of wine. "But to my palate, they lack the mystery that pulls you into pieces like the Blochet."

"The Blochet is fabulous, no argument there,"

Hannah said absently, her mind drawn back to the events of the Gala the week before. She shook her head slightly in wonderment that a scene set with such potential disaster had fizzled before her eyes.

Simona had viewed her precious limestone head without the slightest nod that it was anything other than the same statue that had graced her family's home for four generations. And the odd, high-pitched noise she had made? Well, that, she later explained, was a response to the emotional overload the evening had produced.

That, Hannah thought, or the voice of some very good champagne.

"Today's market is considerably drier than when the Blochet came into circulation," Malcolm was saying, "especially where antiquities are concerned. Governments abroad don't want to see their national treasures end up in private collections."

He fingered a miniature ivory carving from Mycenae while Hannah wondered at the direction the conversation was taking.

"Which makes the piece I have recently acquired," he went on, turning the tiny three-figure grouping in his hand, "all the more enticing. I believe that my latest acquisition will pique everyone's interest this evening."

Hannah felt a rush of blood to her cheeks. Malcolm's invitation had flowed naturally from their conversation at the Gala. And she had assumed the two of them would be dining alone. It now appeared, instead, to be a dinner party, a backdrop for the introduction of an important addition to his already vast collection of art. She glanced down at her beige linen tulip skirt and simple shirt. For what she now understood as an auspicious occasion, she was left horribly underdressed with absolutely no way to remedy the situation. She tugged at the edge of her cropped blouse, hoping it sufficiently met the waistband of her skirt.

"I hope Simona's escort this evening is an art buff," Malcolm was saying. "It will make for a much more interesting table." He turned his attention from the delicately carved ivory figure he had been examining, to Hannah. "And by your expression I take it you didn't know Simona would be joining us at all. I hope this isn't a problem."

"Of course not. You know I enjoy her company," Hannah returned. She puzzled briefly at Simona's failure to mention the invitation before chalking off the minor oddity as an omission befitting a woman of Simona's scattered artistic genius.

There was a gentle rap at the door and Malcolm excused himself. From the living room archway where Hannah stood she recognized Simona's voice and the other, more distinctive one that could only belong to Jesher. She closed her eyes. The pleasant evening was already slipping from her grasp.

To say Jesher's reaction to her had been strained of late was to greatly underplay the facts. Clearly the man could barely tolerate her presence. And why should she expect it to be otherwise? After all, he stolidly believed that she was involved at some level with the disappearance of the Blochet. Hannah twisted the simple gold chain at her throat and wondered if he was always so insolent, or if his disdain was reserved for her alone.

Jesher walked toward Hannah with a graceful gate that spoke of a man at ease with his size and power. "You don't take well to friendly advice, do you," he said when he was well away from his host. A final step drew him entirely too close to her.

"If you're referring to Malcolm," Hannah said and stepped away from his towering presence, "as I recall, it wasn't friendly advice you offered, it was more like a warning." She looked up. Behind delicate frameless glasses, Jesher's green eyes roamed her face with unwarranted possessiveness.

"Either way, you didn't listen," he said easily.

There was a steamy quality to Jesher's voice that reminded Hannah of trench coats and fedoras and foggy back streets way past midnight. She wondered if he knew how much his sultry tone diluted the impact of his message. Or if he cared.

"It's dinner," she said with a casual shrug. "Where's the harm in that?"

Jesher watched the rise and fall of Hannah's shoulders, noting the graceful way she tilted her head like an adjective to the movement. "Ordinarily I would agree with you," he said.

"Ordinarily. But not this time?"

"No," he returned. Then he narrowed his eyes and surveyed his surroundings. At the far end of the living room Malcolm gestured broadly at a piece of Chinese jade while Simona nodded. Evidently satisfied he could not be overheard, Jesher slowly turned his attention back to Hannah. "Hewett is currently unattached," he said quietly. A moment later he added, "and that puts a different spin on the evening."

"Well, thanks for the heads up."

"You're welcome," Jesher returned. Then he picked up a goblet of Riesling and started toward an enormous charcoal, hanging just above a Louis Quatorze love seat.

With a light touch on his jacket sleeve Hannah drew him to a halt.

"We need to talk," she said simply.

Jesher took a contemplative sip of his wine.

"For the past week I've left messages for you every place I could think of," Hannah went on, not caring that his ploy of pauses was a goad to reveal more of her hand. "And you haven't responded. This whole situation has put a strain on my working relationship with your mother." Hannah lowered her voice. "She's mentioned the Gala endlessly this week and several times she asked me how I thought her pieces looked. I don't know how to answer her."

"I've been away."

Hannah bit at her upper lip. Jesher picked over her dialogue like week-old fruit, selecting what he would respond to and leaving the rest to rot.

"You were away," she repeated and then nodded in reaffirmation. "I see. Well, tell me, did you get any leads on the real – "

"This isn't the time or the place." Jesher's words sliced over hers with uncharacteristic speed.

"Then when?" Hannah pressed.

"I'll drive you home," he said and fired a warning glance over her shoulder. She turned to see Simona and Malcolm bearing down on them.

Simona was dressed in a flowing caftan whose sun-washed palette of florals reverberated in the russet tint applied to her hair earlier that afternoon. She was nothing if not dramatic and her attire this evening assumed an artsy air befitting the purpose of Malcolm's little dinner party. But then Simona, Hannah was just learning, was far more designing than her flighty affect would lead one to believe.

"I was just telling Malcolm," Simona said when she was still several feet away, "why I asked Jesher to accompany me this evening, dear." She walked straight to Hannah, took her hand in a gesture of warm affection and gave her a kiss on the cheek. Behind her Malcolm rolled a slow sip of wine across his tongue before swallowing. Something in his expression said he was not pleased with Simona's choice of escorts.

Hannah fingered a curling tendril of her hair that had slipped from its French braid. Perhaps Jesher was right; perhaps Malcolm had plans for the two of them. With a solitary shake of her head, she brushed the thought aside. They were not alone, she and Malcolm.

Simona and Jesher were there. And Jesher was driving her home. What could be safer than that?

"I am always interested in your acquisitions, Malcolm," Jesher was saying. "Wouldn't miss this one for the world. So tell me," he said and smiled coolly, "do you have a buyer lined up?"

Simona swung around to her host. Swirls of orange and red and yellow chased her. "Good grief," she said, "I hope you're not planning to sell." She turned back to her son. "I know it's your livelihood, dear, but selling art is plainly unimaginative. Don't you agree Malcolm?" Then, without giving her host the opportunity to respond she continued. "But when you trade, you must know your own hand as well as your opponent's, or you risk a bad burn. Trading," she said with a reverence reserved for profound disclosures, "now, that's a game. And games make life so much more interesting. Don't you agree, Malcolm?"

But a gentle rap at the door drew Malcolm away before he could respond. Moments later he returned with a tall blond at his side. Hannah closed her eyes briefly and wished to be anywhere but where she was. Next to her host was Lily Kenyon, Jesher's half sister.

Lily was a product of Jesher's father, Alistair Kenyon's wandering ways. Her identity might forever have remained a secret but for the tragic intervention of fate, which left her motherless when she was five. Alistair had brought her to his home to live with Jesher and Simona, and to be raised as a Kenyon. But according to Simona, Lily had never been a good fit. It was a simple case of nature over nurture, Simona had said on more than one occasion. Lily had no interest in the arts, any of them. Instead she had become a banker and, in her spare time, she preferred digging in gardens and the like.

Dinner was served in the library. With no apology for the imposed intimacy, Malcolm led the small party past the formal dining room and through the adjacent sitting room to a set of oak pocket doors, which opened to the library. A small mahogany dining table and matching armchairs had been placed there just for the occasion. The goblets were crystal, the china bone, and the rows of silver flatware that trailed from the plate in either direction promised a meal with more courses than a week had days.

"I've started work on a new piece, everyone," Simona announced when the curried pumpkin soup had been served. She paused for all the attention and when it was hers, basked momentarily in the spotlight of her own making. "It's to be a large statue, using a new medium."

"A new medium?" Malcolm said. "Did Italy finally run out of Carrera?"

Simona quieted his sarcasm with a careless wave of her hand. At her wrist, three heavy gold bangles chimed their response. "I'm calling it, *Collector of Life*."

"It's good, you trying new things," Jesher said. "Too much familiarity makes people stale." He shifted his large frame in his chair, a movement which brought him momentarily closer to Hannah. Tonight, as was often the case, her clothes gave the appearance of form following function. And he might have bought the package, except he remembered how she had looked night of the Gala, how the gentle swell of her breasts curved above her black sequined gown, how they rose and fell with each breath. His eyes closed briefly as he imagined trailing kisses down that soft tawny skin.

"Well, stale I'm not. I feel positively electrified," Simona replied. "It's like the first blush of a new love, fresh and exciting." She picked up her spoon and by turn, assessed the impact of her words on each person seated with her.

"*Collector of Life*," Malcolm said and templed his fingers while he pondered the name. "And what will this *Collector* look like?"

Simona put her hand lightly on Malcolm's. "What I'm working on is symbolic. It is form without detail, a story without words. It's to be a female figure, Earth Mother, if you will. With arms circled to gather in the fruits of her labor, she embraces the centuries-old northern European concept of the female as the life-giving force in the universe. It's a theme I rather prefer to the more Biblical one that sees the seed of man's loins as the source of all life."

Hannah focused on her chilled soup and wondered how a woman of such flowing verbiage could have given birth to a son of such incisive speech patterns.

"It's meant as a public piece, of course," Simona

went on. "Something of this proportion cannot be bound by walls." By now Simona's serving of soup was forgotten. "I plan to move it in the center of Lily's herb garden, near the guest house at Pinehurst where Hannah stays. And get rid of that old Hera statue I did eons ago. You really should come by and see it, Malcolm."

From the corner of her eye, Hannah saw Jesher's spoon pause briefly before it completed its journey to his mouth.

"Maybe I will," Malcolm said.

"Of course," Simona continued, "in a year or so it will have a more settled look, all covered with moss and lichen and such." She fingered a band of plaited gold at her wrist. "Still, it's interesting to see a work in progress, don't you think?" She reached across the array of silverware and took Jesher's hand. "You come, too, dear." She patted his hand and her bracelets tinkled in response.

Malcolm wrinkled his nose. "Lichen? What are you working in, hypertufa?"

"Close," Simona returned. "Cement. Cement troweled over a wire mesh form. Cement, because it refuses significant detail."

"Cement," Malcolm repeated slowly.

"Don't be so stuffy, Malcolm," Simona said. "I know it's considered a poor man's medium, but it's just the break I need from chinking away at limestone and the like. That's it, then," she said and placed her hand lightly on the fine wool of Malcolm's suit jacket, "you'll drop by to see my lady. And let me know when, so Hannah's sure to be there. We'll all have tea. It'll be fun."

The conversation lulled momentarily while Malcolm's server placed plates of poached salmon and steamed spring vegetables before each guest. Though the affection Simona felt for her son was evident, clearly her relationship with Malcolm was more. Their easy banter spoke of chasms of personal contrasts repeatedly spanned by friendship.

Even Jesher seemed in tune with the tone his mother and Malcolm had set. His serious expression lightened a bit and when Malcolm told a very bad, very old joke about an English art dealer and the Mona Lisa, Hannah swore she heard Jesher chuckle. Another evening filled with disaster potential seemed to be turning out well.

"Did you know, Hannah dear, that Malcolm and I share a bit of family history?" Simona said as a sliver of Malcolm's own almond cheesecake was placed in front of her.

Next to Hannah, Jesher warned off his mother's conversational turn with a solitary shake of his head.

Simona lofted a perfectly arched brow at her son and continued, undaunted. "Why, yes. It seems that Malcolm, here, is the great grand nephew of Kenneth Powell."

Hannah had no idea what the connection was between Kenneth Powell and Simona Poole Kenyon, but the darkening look in Jesher's eyes said let the subject drop.

"Coffee?" Malcolm asked after a moment. "Or a brandy?"

"Brandy," Jesher replied. "Hannah?"

"Coffee for me, please," she said.

"And do you know who Kenneth Powell is, Hannah?" Simona continued.

Next to her Jesher drew in a long breath and let it out by degrees.

"I've no idea," Hannah said, "but I'm sure he must be a fascinating character." She paused at the brink of a dangerous chasm before plunging ahead. "Please, tell me more."

Jesher's eyes pounced on her.

Hannah looked away. And smiled. Evidently Jesher did not take well to being crossed. She had heard as much. Well, she didn't much care for his dictatorial ways.

"He was an art dealer." Simona took a bite of her cheesecake and closed her eyes, as if savoring the taste. "And he was friends, some say, with my great grandfather, Richard Woolley."

"I'm sure Hannah is not interested in the in's and out's of the Pooles and the Hewetts, Mother," Jesher said. Then with barely a pause, he added, "You ready to show us what you've got, Malcolm?"

Simona sniffed elegantly at the abrupt closure her son had delivered to the conversation.

"I suppose I have made you wait long enough," Malcolm said. Then he stood and after fishing a small key from his trousers pocket walked to the far corner of the room where he unlocked a panel exposing a touchpad. He entered a series of numbers, which set in motion a section of the library wall. Noiselessly the wall slid away to reveal the barred entrance to a vault.

Despite the age of the house, the closet sized vault sported the latest in technology. From where Hannah was seated, it appeared that Malcolm needed both fingerprint identification and number code to gain entrance. And as soon as that was accomplished, the paneled library wall once again slid into place, leaving Malcolm and his treasures hidden from sight.

Moments later Malcolm emerged carrying an object no more than twelve inches in length, wrapped in a black velvet cloth. With one hand he carefully unfolded the cloth and let the edges slowly slide away from his treasure.

Jesher leaned forward in his chair.

"Stunning," Simona said and peered into the sculpted marble portrait face Malcolm was holding.

Malcolm smiled. Clearly he was enjoying his moment of glory. "Mid fifth century. Of course much later than the Blochet, but interesting in its own right, don't you think?"

He moved to Hannah who could only gape in awe. The sculpture he held was rare and without flaw. The elongated face and shallow engraved lines that formed the features lent a saintly appearance as if the man were, at that moment, transfixed in religious ecstasy.

"Do you know who he was?" Hannah asked.

"An official of the State. But his name?" Malcolm shook his head. "I've no idea." As he spoke, he moved from guest to guest like a first grade teacher holding up a picture book, or a priest serving the Elements.

"Early Christian, then," Jesher said more for himself.

"Or Byzantine, although the distinction is academic."

"How were you able to secure such a piece?" Simona asked and strained for one final look even as Malcolm refolded the velvet cloth about the sculpture.

"It took more than a year," Malcolm said. "As for how," he allowed a smile to play across his perfectly formed lips, "that too, is academic, isn't it? The sculpture is mine. That's what matters, after all."

"Then you plan to keep it?" Simona asked.

"For now."

"You should display it so you can enjoy the returns of your hard work," Hannah said. "How could you stand to keep such beauty locked away for no one to enjoy but you?"

Malcolm allowed his eyes to settle slowly on Hannah's face. "It's not always prudent to share beauty. Besides, there are insurance adjustments that must come first." He plucked the key from his pocket again. "So for the time being, the sculpture must remain in my vault. Now please, enjoy your brandy," he said and turned toward the vault.

"Hannah has to leave and I have offered to drive her home," Jesher said and returned his empty brandy snifter to the table. "Mother, you stay and have a good time. Malcolm's car can bring you when you're ready."

Nearby the metal vault door clanked.

Simona's lips pursed briefly before she smoothed them into a light smile. "I wish you could stay, both of you. I've hardly seen you since the Gala, Jesher."

Jesher glanced automatically at his watch. "It's late. Another time." He stood, and with a look, tugged Hannah to her feet as well.

Moments later Malcolm emerged from his closeted vault. "Surely you're not leaving so soon," he said.

"Afraid so," Jesher returned without offering even the most cursory of excuses. Instead he thanked his host, placed his hand on Hannah's elbow and steered her toward the front door.

Outside, the late April air had turned chilly and what had felt refreshingly cool as they left the house soon sent a shiver racing across Hannah's shoulders. She rubbed at her bare arms and glanced about the circular brick driveway for Jesher's car.

"I'm parked there," Jesher said, his hand still lightly at Hannah's arm. "Behind Malcolm's Jag."

What Hannah saw was a Land Rover. But this was not the plush sport utility vehicle driven by soccer moms. This machine had the face of an army jeep and the soul of a truck.

"Interesting," she said, refusing the taunt Jesher was dangling. "And vintage, too."

"I got used to them overseas. They're no things of beauty, but they are dependable. And, you can take them down to the tires with nothing more than a screwdriver."

"If one had to," Hannah said, though clearly she couldn't imagine why anyone would need to dismantle an entire vehicle.

"Auto repair shops are in short supply in the veldt," Jesher said. "It's a handy skill to have."

Hannah took a turn around the machine. It was charming in an ugly sort of way. It was an open affair with a canvas roof that peeled back like a sardine can. The body was painted a utilitarian green and it sported lugged tires that appeared adequate for mowing down the occasional rhino. "Have you ever done it?" she asked and inclined her head in the direction of the Land Rover. "Taken it apart?"

"To the frame."

"With a screwdriver?"

"Yes."

"In the veldt?"

"In my driveway."

Hannah paused her hand on the door handle and turned back to Jesher. The picture he had just drawn for her refused to work. Why would anyone dismantle an entire truck in one's driveway? Then she stopped herself. She was thinking like a female. "Just to see if you could?"

"Something like that."

Jesher put his hand on the door handle in front of him, and for just a moment, there in the April moonlight, Hannah thought she saw him smile.

"You're welcome to take it for a spin," he said. "If not, your seat's on this side. This Rover was made in England. Right hand drive." Then he opened the door and waited while she climbed inside.

The vehicle's interior was as starkly utilitarian as its exterior. The owners of such types of transportation evidently shunned the courtesies of carpeted floors and window glass and such. The seat padding was wafer thin and promised to be useless if the driver hit anything larger than a dime on the pavement. But Hannah wasn't about to be undone by a vehicle that guaranteed not only a bumpy ride but a cold one as well. She hiked her slim skirt up to her knees and climbed into her ride home.

"Comfy?" Jesher asked when she had smoothed down her skirt.

His tone annoyed her. If he had actually cared about the comfort of his passengers – either his mother or her – he would never have chosen this underdressed stab at a vehicle for his transportation this evening. "Peachy," she returned and smiled broadly at him through the window opening where glass should have been.

Jesher shut the door. For a long moment he studied her. A light breeze lifted the stray curls around her face and pushed them softly across her cheeks. In reply to the cool night air, she shivered.

"You're cold," he told her.

"It's a short ride to Pinehurst."

Jesher took off his suit jacket and handed it to her

through the open window. "Here," he said. Then he walked to the driver's side and got in the Rover.

Hannah wanted to toss the jacket right on his lap. She didn't much like being told what to do with things of a personal nature and it seemed to her that Jesher spent a lot of time doing just that. As if he knew her. As if she were his protégée. She curled her fingers into the woolen fabric of his coat and turned down a sulk.

In her hand, the fabric still radiated heat from his body. And the soft scent of his soap drifted to her nostrils. It was unnervingly intimate.

"Well, aren't you going to put it on?" he said and turned the key in the ignition. The machine shuddered to life. "It won't do you any good if you leave it on your lap."

Hannah didn't trust herself to respond. Instead she picked up the coat, slipped it over her shoulders and leaned back against the hard seat. At her hip she felt something snap. She reached into the jacket pocket and retrieved Jesher's glasses, one earpiece hanging at a crazy angle.

Jesher took them from her hand and tossed them on the console. "It's fine," he offered before she could apologize. "They're just for headaches and they don't really help."

Moments later the Land Rover had cleared the driveway and was on the open road. Brisk night air poured through the glassless orifices of the vehicle, swirling about its interior like a vortex. Hannah ignored the unpleasant chill. She needed to know what

Jesher had found out about the Blochet and judged she had about fifteen minutes to do so before he deposited her at her door.

Carefully she broached his silence. "What a wonderful find Malcolm made in that portrait head," she said hoping he would fly with her opener.

"I'd like to know what he traded to get it," Jesher returned.

"You don't think he paid cash for it, I take it."

Jesher shook his head. "Anyone who would have a piece like that isn't interested in cash, American or otherwise. They only negotiate in kind." He stopped at an intersection and waited while a delivery truck crossed in front of them. "Especially if the provenance is in order. And I'm assuming it is or Malcolm wouldn't be showing it off. Besides," he added after shifting into second gear, "Malcolm doesn't have that kind of disposable income."

"What would it take to get a piece like that on the open market?"

"There is no open market for a piece like that. But it would take something of immense prestige, that or something of personal interest to the other party. In either case, you'd have to know the owner to know what would float his boat."

"Something like, say, the Blochet?"

Jesher chuckled. Hannah was certain of it.

"They're not even in the same class. The Blochet would fetch much more in the art world than any fifth century portrait head from Byzantium."

"Which brings – "

" – you to your next question. What have I found out about the Blochet?"

"Right."

"Nothing," Jesher said and put on his directional signal. "It's as if the theft never happened."

Hannah pulled the jacket more tightly around her to ward off the evening air. "Do you think that's possible? I mean, do you think it just looked different because it was in a different place or because the lighting was different?"

"Not a chance. You and I both know the Blochet is gone."

"I could be wrong," she said.

A smile fleeted across Jesher's lips. But not before Hannah caught it.

"What's funny about that?"

But Jesher had retreated into his well-known Kenyon silence.

It took Hannah only a moment to see what was happening. "You think I'm baiting you, don't you? You still have it in your head that I'm somehow involved in the disappearance of the Blochet. You as much as said it that night in your office and it's obvious that you haven't changed your mind." She stopped speaking for a moment and eyed him carefully. His face was void of expression, as if she hadn't spoken. Hannah felt the rush of blood to her cheeks, driven there by anger. "Frankly," she started up after a moment, "I find your innuendos of my guilt insulting. Do you have any idea how incredibly stupid I would have to be to steal an artifact like the Blochet when it had been entrusted into my personal care? And then alert you to the fact that it was gone?"

Of course Jesher didn't respond, not that Hannah actually thought he would. Instead he pulled the Land Rover to a halt at the gate to Pinehurst, the Poole estate.

Beside him Hannah seethed. Jesher Kenyon was arrogant and impossible and at this moment she didn't blame Savatheda Christiana one bit for seeking friendlier pastures.

Leaning unceremoniously across Hannah, Jesher hit four numbers on a metal keypad just outside her window and waited while the double wrought iron gates slid slowly back. Then he leaned back, kicked the truck into first gear and chugged onto the grounds.

"I did not take the reserve head," Hannah said again.

"Good," he told her and aimed a smile in her direction. "That eliminates one suspect."

"Then you believe me?"

Jesher shifted into second gear.

"No, you don't. I can tell." In her lap, her short nails dug into the soft flesh of her palms as she made tight fists.

Jesher pulled the Land Rover to a halt half way to the main house, dumped his smile and looked directly at his passenger. "The jury's still out on what I believe," he said. Beside him Hannah stared straight ahead.

Jesher surveyed his passenger. Frustration, or anger, had drawn tight the beautiful contours of her face and had straightened her lips into a thin line. And she shivered. Despite the protection his suit coat offered, Hannah shivered. "You're still cold," he said, his voice nothing more than a whisper.

"I'm fine."

"Of course you are," he said. "My mistake." Then he pushed the stick shift into gear and aimed the Land Rover toward the guesthouse.

"So what do I tell Simona when she asks me again about the Blochet, because she's already asked several times?"

"Tell her it looked great and change the subject."

"You want me to put on an act for your mother?"

Jesher pulled the Land Rover up to the front of the guesthouse and killed the engine. He turned slowly to the small woman beside him. Her lips were still parted in a question, exposing a row of even teeth. "You and I have already had a conversation about acting and my mother."

The words prodded Hannah like a finger to the ribs. She started to reply but thought better of it, choosing instead simply to leave. She yanked down the handle pushing the door at the same time. It creaked in protest but it didn't budge. "Perfect," she muttered and pushed again. Nothing happened. At that moment she would have crawled through the open window rather than ask for help. She bit down on her lower lip and leaned away from the door, preparing to throw her shoulder into it.

"You have to hit it here," Jesher said with great calm, and reaching across her, smacked the door soundly with his fist. Immediately it sprang open.

Hannah stepped out. "Thanks for the ride," she said and slammed shut the door with as much power as she could muster.

In reply, the entire vehicle shuddered. Jesher smiled and watched her walk to the cottage door, every muscle in her body indignantly taut.

In a half dozen strides he was at her side.

At her doorway she stopped and turned to him. "What now?" she fired out. The night air tugged at the edges of his hair, lifting it and letting it go to settle again as if had never moved.

"My jacket."

He meant simply to pluck the garment from her shoulders and be on his way. But though the night was warm, Hannah was cold and he suddenly wanted her not to be. Later, he told himself, he would sort through his actions and coat them with rationality until they became sweet enough to swallow. Later. But right now all he wanted to do was kiss this woman who was bright and beautiful and maybe the cleverest thief he had ever met.

With calculated casualness he hooked a finger beneath her chin and lifted her face toward his. He caught a fleetingly quizzical look in her eyes before he closed his and gave in to his sentient desires.

She tasted sweet. Sweet and soft. And her lips were unexpectedly pliant against his. He put one arm around her waist tugging her close so he could feel the press of her breasts against him. She was smaller in his arms than he had imagined she would be, though not in the least frail. With effort he lifted his mouth from hers and pulled at the air in a long, deep breath.

Then without regret for what he had just done, he opened his eyes and awaited his fate. He expected her to protest, righteously enraged. She was, after all, his mother's personal assistant, not his date, and theirs was but a professional relationship.

Hannah Swift did nothing of the kind. Instead she wrapped her arms about him, mindless of his Armani suit jacket that now lay in a heap on the chiseled stones of her entryway. He was warm, this man, and his heat warmed her. She shivered again, but this time not from the chill April air.

Jesher pressed her against the door and inclined his head, licking at the edges of her lips until he heard her groan and when she did, he slipped his tongue inside. Her mouth was warm and wet and waiting for him as if she had known all along how it would be. He shuddered and drove deeper into her, blinded with a need to fill her with himself.

He pushed her harder against the door, pressing himself between her legs, wanting to be in a place he didn't dare. And then when he could bear no more of the sweet torment he had imposed on himself, he tasted her one last time and slowly released her shoulders.

"Christ," he muttered. He was grateful for the darkness, grateful that this woman could not see what she had done to him.

Hannah leaned against her door and tugged in a ragged breath. Then she ran the tip of her tongue over her lips, tasting him one final time. Her cheeks were flushed; she could feel the heat in them and her heart was pounding as if she just finished a race. She didn't even try to read his face. He was the master of inscrutability. Instead she waited for her breath to come. "Where," she asked when she had found her voice, "did that come from?"

Jesher straightened away from her and swallowed hard, willing control back into his body. With his fingers he raked back his hair while his eyes worked over her face, pausing at her lips now swollen from his desire. He blinked deeply once and slowly shook his head.

"I have no idea," he said at last.

CHAPTER FOUR

Hannah breathed a sigh of relief when she heard Jesher's voice on the phone. Marlene McGuire, Jesher's executive assistant, had a laundry list of stock answers, which she used to fend off callers. Unavailable. Away from his desk. With a client. But today Jesher had answered.

"There's something you need to see," she said. Then added, "This is Hannah."

"What is it, Hannah?"

His tone was warm, welcoming. Hannah wondered that he was ever able to close a business deal when his voice sounded like an invitation to bed. Then again, maybe it just seemed that way to her. Maybe to other people he merely sounded hoarse. "It would be easier to show you," she answered.

"Can you come by?"

"No," she told him.

"Then I'll come to you. Where are you?"

His easy acquiescence surprised her. For a heartbeat she didn't answer. "I'm at the guesthouse," she said finally. "But it's not here. It's in your mother's studio.

"Give me twenty minutes," he said and disconnected.

In much less time than that, Hannah heard tires on the gravel road that wound through the Poole estate. She opened the guesthouse door and headed toward

Jesher before he had even cut the engine.

"This is important. I never would have called if it weren't," Hannah began.

A rush of icy air followed Jesher as he left the car. It clung momentarily to his clothes before sifting into the late morning warmth.

"I went to tell Simona about my plans to leave but she wasn't around. I finally found her near the herb garden working on her new piece, *Collector of Life*." Hannah felt a flush rise to her cheeks when she glanced up at the man who had so completely caught her off guard with his kiss. He wore faded jeans, slung low on his lean, narrow hips and a tan T-shirt with Casey's Bar emblazoned on the front. Only his immaculately scissored hair gave any hint that he was something other than a laborer. That, and the Jaguar he drove.

Jesher leaned back against the fender and waited.

"Simona doesn't like being distracted when she's working. You probably know that. And when she finally looked down at me from her ladder, she asked me to get her a trowel from the studio. The one with the blue handle. She was very specific."

Hannah's cheeks were deep with color the way they had been the night he kissed her, Jesher noted with less disinterest than he had hoped. That night he had figured to catch her off guard, to take her mouth swiftly before she raised a protest and then to leave, his curiosity about the incredible softness of her lips finally satisfied.

Instead, the surprise had been on him.

And while his curiosity was temporarily satisfied, his need to know more of this woman was not.

"Did you say you have a key," Hannah was saying. "I can't remember."

Jesher's eyes touched her cheeks and chin before settling quietly on her lips. Beneath his gaze she shifted.

"To the studio?" she added.

Jesher nodded. "Does Mother know you've been snooping around?"

Hannah's head came up sharply. "She asked me to run an errand for her. She gave me the key. I wasn't snooping. Weren't you listening?"

"You're not leaving Mother's employ," he said simply. "I was listening."

Hannah narrowed her eyes. He was picking through her conversation again. This time, her planned departure had evidently caught his fancy. "This is not about my leaving. This is about the Blochet."

"You're staying on until this theft is settled."

"Well, that's what I'm trying to do right now. Get it settled. If you would just look at what I found." Hannah reined in her exasperation and waited for a response.

"After you," Jesher said.

A short walk through a planted stand of ancient pines brought them to the studio near the rear of the property. Jesher fitted the small brass key into the lock and waited for the door to swing open. It was dark inside, even with the skylights which Simona had recently added. Jesher flipped a switch and the single room sprang into view.

"It's over here," Hannah said and indicated a corner. Around the studio were work tables belonging to the few students Simona had agreed to mentor. On several of the tables unfinished sculptures were covered with sheets. Art in progress, no matter what the medium, was covered as a matter of course to keep it from critics' eyes.

Jesher ambled over, his very gait indicative of the weight he lent to Hannah's apparent find. "If it's draped, Hannah, you should leave it alone," Jesher said.

"It isn't," she replied. "And I don't think Simona would mind anyway, given the stakes. She reached for a piece of limestone that had been meticulously carved. "Remember I said she had been working on a study?" She turned around with the limestone block in her hand and met a wall of man. Jesher Kenyon had noiselessly crossed the room and with subtle overbearance had invaded her space. She swallowed and held up the limestone sculpture for him to see.

"A mouth," Jesher noted almost absently. "Yours is softer."

Hannah raised her chin. "It's your mother's study of the Blochet mouth and don't tell me you didn't recognize it."

Jesher took off his glasses and rubbed his eyes.

"It's startling, the resemblance," Hannah said.

"Mother's good." He shrugged. "She trained with the best. What's your point?"

"Look at it more closely. The edge of the lower lip. Just here." Hannah turned the sculpture in Jesher's hand to show him what she meant.

A familiar citrusy scent floated up to Jesher and he inhaled it greedily. It was soap, or shampoo, something Hannah used every day. It was a scent he could remember if he closed his eyes. He felt his body tighten and willed it to stop.

Hannah took a small chisel from his mother's toolbox. "This," she said and held out the instrument, "is your mother's. It has her initials on it. It also has a break in the blade. Here, I'll show you." She took his hand. "Feel that?" she said and ran the blade lightly over his forefinger.

Jesher's eyes blinked briefly shut. "Do it again," he said.

Hannah ignored the sensuality he had intended and once more ran the blade over the sensitive tip of his finger. "Anything?"

Hannah waited, expecting another verbal parry that seemed his style today.

"There's a catch in it," he said eventually.

"Exactly. Making small imperfections." She turned the limestone about in his hand. "See, here. And again here?"

"It's a study, Hannah," he said and held out the sculptured mouth for her to take. "They're often not finished. I'm not surprised it's not smooth."

Hannah nodded. "There are no tool marks like this on the real Blochet."

Jesher's eyes stopped roving hungrily over Hannah. He held the study up to the light and turned it carefully in his hand. "And you saw these marks on the head at the Vic?" he asked after a moment. "Is that what you're saying?"

"I can't be positive," Hannah said.

Jesher held the limestone block out for Hannah to take. Then he shook his head. "This is just a study of the Blochet mouth. Nothing more."

Hannah carefully replaced the chisel in Simona's toolbox and then put the limestone study back where she had found it.

"Artists don't share their tools. I know because I don't share mine. These instruments," she pointed to the Simona's metal box, "have special meaning and value. They are highly personal, highly prized."

"It doesn't mean anything," Jesher returned.

"It could."

But Jesher was again shaking his head. "If the Blochet at the Vic has similar marks, it only means that this tool, or one like it, was used. It's like owning a gun. Just because it's yours, it doesn't mean you pulled the trigger."

"But you could have. And it would certainly make you the most likely suspect." The words tumbled from Hannah. "Knowing if this chisel was used on the copy of the Blochet would call up a narrow list of suspects."

"Possibly." Jesher squinted through the light that

had now begun to flood the room.

Hannah turned away.

As he watched, her shoulders heaved in a sigh of apparent exasperation. "You're upset," he said. His voice was suddenly soft, barely audible.

"Frustrated," she said. "I've found something here and you won't admit it. You've already convinced yourself that I am involved, and you've closed yourself off to any other explanations."

"Not true." With the tips of his fingers he rubbed at his temple, then walked out of the square of sunlight spreading on the floor, and into a darker place.

"Jesher, I'm not accusing your mother, I'm trying to get to the bottom of this mess."

"And clear yourself."

"Why not? Even if Simona didn't carve the Blochet that's in the Vic, chances are good that whoever did has convenient access to her tools. And that means it's probably someone who sculpts here."

"That makes sense."

He raked his fingers through his hair, and as Hannah watched, the neatly clipped strands of glossy, chocolate colored hair fell back into place. "Good, I'm glad you see things my way," she said.

"That isn't what I said. There's a short list of people familiar enough with the Blochet and talented enough to make a copy. You're not a sculptor."

"That lets me off the hook?"

"That moves you to the back burner."

A reprieve, if only temporary, gave Hannah the

impetus to share her plan. "I'm driving to Toronto this afternoon and check out the Blochet, see if it has the same kind of markings. Then we'll know a lot more."

"Not today." He said it like an order.

"On my own time, of course," she added. "After work."

"The Vic would be closed by the time you got there. Besides, I'm going with you."

"Because you want to see for yourself? Or because you don't trust me out of the country?"

A cool smile was Jesher's only response.

***

Hannah had gotten up early to complete her work for Simona before Jesher arrived. Simona had given her space – a desk, a chair and a computer – in one of the small rooms just off the foyer of the main house. Now Hannah closed Simona's planner and focused her attention on the large older man who had just entered the foyer.

His name was Alistair Kenyon and he was an imposing figure. If Hannah had given him much thought, she would have expected nothing less. Of course there were no pictures of him at Pinehurst, at least none in the public spaces. But Hannah suspected that when Simona had ceremoniously stripped the visible memories of her husband from the estate, she had tucked them carefully away. Simona could not bear to dispose of anything. Not even, it appeared, once-loved husbands.

He was tall, this father of Jesher Kenyon, but his face was quieter than his son's. Cheekbones, angular jaw, patrician nose – all were there. But time, or a gentler view of life, had erased the stark quality Jesher wore.

His charm was subtle, a half smile quickly gone, a touch on the elbow, a shift in the stance that closed the distance between him and his former wife. And the charm worked. As Hannah watched, Simona Poole Kenyon, the woman who was constructing her version of Everywoman from welded rods and cement, became suddenly kittenish. A hand went to her hair, brushing it from her eyes. Then she looked up at him through her thick fringe of dark lashes. "Alistair," she managed, finally.

Alistair inclined his head and, taking her hands, kissed her lightly on both cheeks. It could have been a European gesture of greeting, except that there was a subtle sensuality to the way he let the length of him linger against Simona.

Simona blushed.

Hannah stood and in so doing, raked the legs of the chair across the tiled floor.

"Hannah," Simona called. Her voice sounded mildly startled. "I want you to meet someone."

Dutifully Hannah walked to the foyer, apprehensive of this man's charm as though, if he but chose to do so, he could work his magic on her.

Up close, Alistair Kenyon was flawlessly

attractive. As handsome, no doubt, as he had been the day he married Simona. Though tall and broad shouldered like his son, he bore none of Jesher's abrupt aggression. But like his son, his movements were smooth and calm, a man used to his own skin and needing to prove nothing.

He took her hand but rather than shake it, held it in a gesture reserved for a warm acquaintance.

"This is Hannah Swift, my personal assistant. She's such a treasure," Simona said. "She keeps track of everything for me so I can focus on my art."

Alistair still held Hannah's hand between his. "How long have you been with the family?"

His eyes were green, like May grass. Like Jesher's. Hannah fought a rush of blood to her cheeks. "Almost two years," she said. "I've enjoyed working here."

"That sounds as if you're leaving," Alistair said.

"I have been up front about my desire eventually to pursue a career as an art curator. Now the time may be right for me to think about moving on."

"Nonsense," Simona said. "You'll stay here. We'll talk. But later. Right now I have a house guest."

It sounded as if the visit would extend through more than the afternoon. A glance to the foyer proved Hannah right. Two beat up duffle bags lay crumpled by the door, a bevy of paper airline identification tags still choking their worn leather handles.

Hannah worried at the luggage, worried at the situation. That Jesher had little truck with his father was no family secret. This was a man who had bedded numerous women while Simona was his wife and had fathered Lily by one of those affairs. If there were others, no one in the family gave them voice.

Jesher likely did not know of his father's return, or of his apparent plans to stay on. It was also likely that when he found out, he wouldn't be pleased. What Hannah needed to do was postpone that revelation until after their trip to Toronto. Common sense said the trek would be more bearable if Jesher's mood wasn't fouled by the likes of Alistair.

A sound came from the circular driveway beyond.

Simona shifted to look past Alistair, then settled her eyes on Hannah. Though her voice seemed as quiet as ever, a blush of color had taken her cheeks. "Do you and Jesher have plans?" she asked.

"Business," Hannah said.

"Is that what it's called now?" Simona said.

"I'll be away from my desk for the rest of the day. I left the information for you on your email."

Simona gave her hand a careless wave. "I never check it."

"I also left a note pinned to the front pocket of your overalls."

"That's more like it."

Hannah heard the car door shut. In a matter of seconds Jesher would be at the door. And in a matter of a few more, the fireworks would begin. She looked for her keys, hoping to head him off.

But it was already too late.

Jesher pulled back the screen door and stepped

into the foyer. In a familial stance that had become all too familiar to Hannah, Alistair stood his ground.

The air chilled noticeably.

"Dad," was all Jesher said.

His father's face softened visibly. "It's good to see you, son. It's been a while. Too long."

Jesher didn't reply. Instead he looked past his parents to the luggage mounded in the corner. "Mother," he said by way of greeting and, leaning past his father, lightly kissed her cheek. Then he turned to Hannah. "I'll be in the car," he told her and stepped back into the bright afternoon.

Hannah hurried through her goodbyes and followed Jesher moments later, relieved to be rid of the awkward situation just inside the doors of Pinehurst.

Outside the air was fresh and sweet. Hannah glanced about for Jesher's Land Rover. But today he had opted for a more civilized approach to their trip. Today he had driven the black Jaguar.

The engine was already humming, and as she approached the passenger side Jesher leaned over and popped the door.

Inside the car was frigid. Despite the pleasant spring day, Jesher had the air conditioning churning. Too late for sweaters or jackets. Jesher was anxious to leave and she was unwilling to test the ragged edge of his decent nature. She must have looked desperate, or at least chilled because Jesher touched a control panel, and first the fan, and then the air conditioning hummed to a halt.

"Thank you," she said.

They were halfway to the front gate when a truck rounded the curve speeding toward them and kicking up dust from the crushed stone.

"That looks like my brother's truck. I wonder what he's doing here."

"Let's ask him," Jesher replied and stopped his car squarely in the middle of the narrow gravel drive.

Turner lay on the horn but in the end was forced to pull his beat-up machine to a halt. Before Hannah could unfasten her seatbelt, her brother was out of the truck and swaggering toward the driver's side of the Jag.

Hannah held her breath. It was impossible to tell from Jesher's tone how bound he was by anger. But she knew Turner. It didn't take much to bring his macho side front and center. And the last thing she wanted to witness was a pissing match between her brother and her employer.

Jesher rolled down the window, letting the last of the cool air escape. Beyond the open space, Turner's pale eyes tightened. He stood beside the car, motionless, except for his chest, which heaved with barely contained anger. His rigid stance held a primitive dare.

Turner slapped his hand soundly on the roof of the Jaguar. "Are you crazy, man?" he said. "Why the hell couldn't you move over?" He refused to dignify his question with the civility of eye contact. Instead he remained upright, giving Jesher only a view of his well-endowed crotch. Hannah couldn't help but think it was yet one more manifestation of her brother's view of self.

"This is private property," Jesher returned, his voice never rising to the overt display of machismo. "How did you get past the gate?"

Turner cocked his head but refused to respond. "I'm here to see my sister," he said instead. He still stood rigidly by the car, refusing to lean in toward its occupants. "That O.K. with you?"

"What's not O.K. is barreling down the driveway. Ease up on the gas."

Turner had turned to head back to his truck when Jesher added, "Your sister is right here."

Turner pivoted slowly and peered through the window. "Hey Hannah," he said across Jesher. "We have to talk."

"Call me this evening. Mr. Kenyon and I have a long drive ahead of us."

"No can do," Turner said. "This can't wait." He shook his head. "Gotta happen now. It's important." He paused and made fleeting eye contact with Jesher. "And private."

Hannah opened the door. "I won't be long," she said over her shoulder to Jesher.

Turner looked scruffier than usual, like he hadn't thought to shower or shave. His long black hair was held from his face in a thick ponytail at the base of his neck. Yet despite the rough appearance, his face was still handsome, his expression endlessly poignant.

There had been a time when he had frequently smiled, but life had been lighter then. Now he was sullen or tired or angry or maybe all of it. Hannah didn't know, and Turner wouldn't say, and it made her sad.

Hannah trailed after him as he walked away from the vehicles toward a stand of pines. "This couldn't wait?" she asked. She knew she sounded annoyed. "That man is my employer. I wasn't on a date."

"I need some cash," Turner said and pulled a cigarette from a well-worn pack in his shirt pocket.

Hannah sagged.

"It's important," he went on. "I told you."

"How much?" Hannah asked.

He tamped the cigarette several times on an ancient Zippo lighter, then returned it, unlit, to the crumpled pack in his pocket. "I need ten, but a couple would be a start." He glanced back at the Jaguar and whistled softly between his teeth. "Cushy wheels. You're doing all right, Sis." His head bobbed up and down like a dashboard hound.

"This is business, Turner. I told you he wasn't my date."

"Well then you must be blind, Hannah, because he's got it written all over his face."

"What, exactly does he have written on his face?" Hannah asked.

"It," Turner said and raised an eyebrow. "Now, about the money?"

Hannah frowned. "I don't have that kind of money sitting around."

"Savings?" Turner suggested with a casual shrug. "They pay you well enough here, would be my guess."

"I have a little bit in my savings. I can get it for you later this week. Maybe tomorrow."

But Turner was already shaking his head. "I need it now."

"I know I promised I wouldn't ask, Turner, but just tell me, are you in some kind of trouble?"

But Turner wouldn't say a word.

Her brother was bleeding her dry. The last time he'd asked for money he had promised that was the end. Now here he was again. "I can't ask Mr. Kenyon to drive me to the bank right now. We have a long ride ahead of us."

"It won't take five," Turner said. "If you're nervous about asking him," he lifted his chin in the direction of the waiting car, "I know I don't mind."

Hannah tried one more time. "He's a busy man, Turner," she said but her brother was already walking back to the car. Before Hannah could intercept him, he tapped on the darkened window glass and when Jesher again lowered it, he stuck his head inside.

"My sister needs you to do a favor for her. You don't mind, do you? Won't take more than ten minutes of your time. Thanks, man," he said before Jesher could respond, and headed back to his truck.

Hannah slid into her seat.

"What kind of favor is it, exactly, that I'm doing for you?" Jesher asked and flipped off the air conditioning again.

"I need to go to the closest branch of First National. My brother needs more money."

CHAPTER FIVE

In fact it took more than an hour for Hannah to get the thousand dollars that Turner so desperately needed. Through it all Jesher hardly spoke. Hannah wondered if he was becoming mellower or if his silence was because of a headache which appeared to be gaining on him.

Eventually Jesher reached for his glasses, slipped them on, and blinked deeply several times as if adjusting to their strength. But as he steered out of the bank parking lot, he took them off again and dropped them casually on the dashboard.

"You have to give them a chance to work," Hannah said. Jesher didn't reply, leaving Hannah to wonder whether he hadn't heard or simply chose not to respond. "Your eyes have to adjust to the glasses," she said. "If you give them a chance, they'll work. But you have to wear them all the time."

Jesher's eyes left the road, pinning Hannah momentarily against the seat.

"Just a suggestion," she said, refusing to wriggle under his scrutiny. "It's your very own, very personal headache." She crossed her arms beneath her breasts and let out an audible breath.

Jesher reached for his glasses and put them back on.

"They make your eyes ache, don't they?" Hannah offered. "But you'll get used to them and your headaches will go away." She chanced a look in his direction. The muscles in his jaw were working feverishly. Determined that his irritation not steal his tongue, she posed a pointed question. "How long have you had them?"

"A couple of months," he managed with great effort.

"Why that's no time at all. You've got to give them a fair chance. Wear them all the time for the next month. I think you'll be surprised."

"Thank you," Jesher said. His voice was barely audible.

"You're welcome," she responded.

Again Jesher blinked deeply. Then he rubbed the bridge of his nose and started to remove the glasses before he evidently thought better of it and left them where they were.

"How did you get so smart?" he said.

His quiet voice shivered her. If Hannah hadn't attended to his message, she would have sworn he had just issued an invitation to bed her.

"You have wisdom beyond your years," he was saying.

"This has nothing to do with smart. I'm a practical person. If you want something to happen, then you need to take steps to see that it does."

Jesher headed up the ramp that led to the New York State Thruway, downshifting as he eased into the line at the string of tollbooths that guarded the entrance. Hannah glanced over and saw the tightness about his eyes beginning to ease a bit.

"You want your headaches to go away. So you buy the glasses. But you have to wear them. They don't work on your eyes if they are living in your pocket." She absently ran her fingers over her plain brown leather watchband and the discount store watch it held in place. Jesher didn't like taking advice, she would wager. And she doubted he stomached being wrong very well either. But this time he would do both. She knew what she was talking about. Her mother had suffered from horrid headaches – the result of severe astigmatism – until she found relief in glasses. The same would be true of Jesher. She was certain of it.

"And what do you want, Hannah Swift?"

In her seat Hannah turned toward him.

"From life, Hannah. What is it that you want?"

Hannah answered immediately. "I want to pursue my career. It's been my dream since I started college to manage a public gallery, to be able to bring touring exhibits so that people would have a chance to see great art. That's what I want."

Jesher pulled up behind an eighteen-wheeler, waited until the traffic thinned, then sped around it. "You gave that up," he told her. "So it must not have been right for you."

"Oh, it was right for me. But Turner needed help. He's family, I had to do what I could."

Next to her, Jesher nodded. "That's not much to want, just a job."

"A career," she corrected.

"That's it?"

His eyes left the road and found her. Green eyes, pale and pure like an early spring leaf. They pulled her in, these eyes of his, like whirlwind. Like a vortex. Deeper and deeper.

"What about a home, a family of your own?"

"If that happens, yes, of course."

He slipped neatly past another truck, and another before returning to the right-hand lane. As Hannah watched, a clever smile worked its way across his lips. "Didn't you just tell me you don't wait for things to happen, you make them happen?"

"Yes, I did."

"And didn't you just now leave home and family to the fates?"

"I said you can make things happen. But falling in love, that's a different story. It's either in the cards or it isn't. People don't have any control over such things." Her brow furrowed. "I'm surprised you'd even ask."

It was almost four o'clock before they reached Toronto. Traffic on the QEW, the main thoroughfare leading into the city, was heavy. By the time they arrived at the Royal Victoria Museum it was after four thirty. Jesher left his Jaguar parked squarely in front of the imposing stone building without a thought to laws or regulations. Taking Hannah by the elbow, he hurried her into the building.

Five minutes later they were staring into the empty eyes of *L'homme Ordinaire*.

The life-sized head still took her breath away.

Knowing that that a man who actually looked like that had lived, had breathed, had hoped and maybe feared – it awed her.

For Jesher there were more practical considerations. He strolled around the obelisk that held the statuary twice before settling himself squarely in front of it. Then he leaned forward until his patrician nose was but inches from the Plexiglas that enclosed the Blochet.

Hannah was intrigued. His eyes methodically scanned the face, centimeter by centimeter, plotting the face mentally like a graph. As she watched fine lines on his brow first deepened and then smoothed out

"See anything?" he said, his eyes never leaving the sculpted limestone before him.

Hannah forced her attention away from the man at her side and back to the face of the one that had lived thousands of years before. "It's hard to see. There's so much reflection on the Plexiglas. Maybe we could have Dr. Dewald open the case for just a moment."

"Bad idea," was all he said.

And it was. If Dewald even suspected something was amiss with the head it could unleash a whole army of problems. Not to mention the embarrassment it could cause Dewald personally, having curated an exhibit with a fake.

She peered at the head from the side.

"Here," she said suddenly. "Here, just above the lip. What do you think?" She pointed at a small area beyond the heavy plastic casing. When she looked up

Jesher was inches from her face. He had a pencil thin scar, she noticed, that angled across his cheekbone. That tiny mark held a story she would never hear.

She swallowed and stepped away.

Jesher's hand went to the metal bow of his glasses to pull them from his face. Then he evidently caught himself, because he left them where they were.

Hannah let her eyes follow the line of the sculpture back to the ear where the meticulously stylized detail seemed to fade into roughness. Here the marks from a chisel were even more pronounced.

"Jesher," she whispered. "Over here."

He stepped up behind her, blocking the draft from the constantly moving, artificially cooled air. His presence was like a furnace. It was the same heat she had felt when his body had pressed against hers the night of Malcolm's party, the night he had kissed her. She closed her eyes, remembering. The kiss had probably been a foolish moment of weakness from a carefully strong man. But it had left her yearning for more, dreaming about him, all the while knowing it would never be.

"These marks," he said, "are not on the original."

Then she was certain she was right. No matter the mistakes Jesher may have made in his personal life, she knew he would never make one in the world of art. It was his business.

It was his life.

A curling wisp of ebony hair moved with the noiselessly circulating air. Jesher watched it dance about the slim line of Hannah's neck. Practical, she had called herself. And she was right. She had goals, personal benchmarks for achievement in life. Even her clothes were sensible. But there was another side to Hannah Swift, one he would wager lay untapped. She had kissed him back that night, her lips warm and ready, her body fitting smoothly into his. Fire smoldered just below that sensible exterior of hers, waiting for air that would fan its flames. And he wanted to be the one to unleash that fire. Despite the fact that her practical side screamed ordinary, he knew she was not. Despite the fact that she was unlike the other women whose company he had kept, he wanted her. Desperately. And he didn't know what to do about it.

"I suggest," he said, his voice harsh with a yearning he didn't understand, "that we head home. We've seen what we need to see."

And then the heat was gone. Cool mechanized air once more swirled about Hannah, chilling her flesh so recently warmed. She turned and saw Jesher walking toward the door.

***

Someone was talking but Hannah couldn't understand the words. She heard the voice again and this time it sounded like her name. Then someone touched her and she opened her eyes.

"We're home," Jesher said.

Hannah sat up straighter.

"You slept most of the way," he mentioned. "I hope it wasn't the company."

Hannah felt her cheeks darken. "No," she said and shook her head. His eyes were on her, all over her, touching her, caressing her.

"Don't be embarrassed," he said.

"I'm not," Hannah assured him, though her face burned.

"Of course you're not."

Hannah's teeth clamped down hard. She didn't blush. Not ever. Because she didn't do the kinds of things that caused blushing. She was too careful for that. Yet here she was, her cheeks hot with a flush. She squared her shoulders and turned toward the window.

"Are you planning to ask your mother about the chisel?" she said after she cooled.

"Do you have a better idea?" he returned. "The Blochet in the Vic isn't real. We agree on that much. It bears signature marks from a chisel, maybe Mother's. I want answers."

At the gate to Pinehurst, he punched the code into the keypad and waited while the huge iron affair swung open. And just for a moment, he wondered again how Turner had gotten past it.

A short time later, they found Simona in her studio. Though it was too dark to rely on natural light, Simona was hard at work. Before her sat Alistair, smiling his sensuous Kenyon smile while Simona's hand flew about a large sketch tablet.

Jesher shifted his stance and Hannah saw a muscle in his jaw tighten down. His tentative mood fanned into fire by his father's arrival was rapidly darkening. He rapped once on the open door, then entered the spacious room.

Simona barely glanced up. A brief nod acknowledged her son's presence, but her focus was on the work at hand.

Jesher moved quietly behind her and glanced at her sketch. "It's very good, Mother."

Simona nodded, but the smile was for her former husband, and it occurred to Hannah that the real sadness lay in Alistair's ever-errant eye because here, truly, was a love that should have been.

"Your sweet talking came from your father," she said without taking her eyes from the man whose image she was recreating.

To Hannah, Alistair looked less tired, more relaxed than he had when he had arrived. Perhaps he hadn't been sure there would be a place for him at Pinehurst, and now he knew there was. The seedy edge to him was gone as well. Hannah moved away from the door for a better look. New clothes, maybe. Or at least clean. And he had shaved.

"Mother?" Jesher said.

"Hmm?" she responded without turning from her sketchpad.

"Did you make a copy of the Blochet?"

The room filled with a silence that, to Hannah, felt thick and oppressive.

"More or less," Simona answered eventually.

Jesher waited for her to continue and when she didn't he pressed her. "Meaning?"

Simona paused her hand. "Copying is always difficult, Jesher. You know that. Still, capturing the essence of a master's work has always been regarded as a way to refine one's skills."

"Did you finish the sculpture?"

Simona stopped sketching for a moment and looked at her son. "I wasn't pleased with him. I couldn't quite grasp the expression on his mouth. I even made a study of the lips, but . . ." She shook her head. "I just couldn't get him right, you know."

"What did you do with it?" Jesher asked.

The charcoal slipped from Simona's hand to the maple floor where it shattered. At last Alistair rose from the model's stool, retrieved the pieces and pressed them into Simona's hand.

"Oh dear," Simona said. "Am I in trouble?"

CHAPTER SIX

Hannah dropped the visor on the windshield of her car, fastened her seat belt and headed west. Her preliminary interview at the Ashfield Art Gallery in Syracuse had gone very well. It was a small gallery and the assistant curator's position did not pay much, but securing it would start Hannah in the right direction. And she needed to start somewhere or she would never gain enough experience to run a gallery by herself.

At a red light she slipped the director's business card into her purse. He needed letters of reference, he had told her, before he could move on to the next stage of the hiring process. But Hannah knew references wouldn't be easy. The head curator at the Phipps Gallery where she had worked two years earlier had died. The only other position she had held since college was her current one with Simona.

Hannah took the entrance ramp to the New York State Thruway and headed home. She couldn't ask Simona for a reference. The woman was simply too unpredictable. She might not even write the letter and if she did, there was a fifty-fifty chance it would be gibberish. Besides, as Jesher had said, Simona was distracted by Alistair, and no one knew how long he planned to be around.

That left Jesher.

Hannah sighed. Jesher was less familiar with the

various responsibilities she had taken on for Simona, which meant a letter from him would undoubtedly have a generic quality to it. Still, he was her only viable employer and without the letter, generic or not, she stood no chance of being hired.

With a sigh she called Kenyon International. Immediately her call was transferred to Ms. McGuire who said in her typically cool tone that Mr. Kenyon was unavailable.

Hannah shook her head. No surprise there. Despite misgivings, she left her request with his secretary. "You'll be certain he gets the message," Hannah said when she had finished. "It's very important."

"Would you rather leave it on his voice mail?" the woman inquired with a tone that could freeze hell itself.

Hannah told her she would not.

"Since I have you on the line," Ms. McGuire went on, "there is a matter I'm certain you will be able to clear up. It's regarding Mr. Kenyon's mother. Just a moment," she said and pushed the *hold* button. Bach's "Italian Concerto" seamlessly replaced the silence. A moment later Ms. McGuire was back.

"The message is from a Mr. Woodrow at First National."

Automatically Hannah's stomach did a little flip. She had been balancing Simona's personal checking account because if she didn't do it herself, it didn't get done. Now she worried she had made an error.

"Evidently Mrs. Kenyon has initiated a transaction which the bank cannot complete without authorization."

"I can't authorize anything," Hannah said. "I just balance her books. You need to speak to Mr. Kenyon, but as you said, Mr. Kenyon is – "

"Unavailable," Ms. McGuire finished for her. "However, Mrs. Kenyon assured both me and the bank that you could handle it."

"I'll do what I can."

Ms. McGuire recited the bank phone number and followed it with an extension. Her voice softened slightly when she thanked Hannah but she disconnected before Hannah could respond to the kinder tone. Hannah drove on in silence. Mr. Woodrow would have to wait until she got home.

When Hannah opened her cottage door an hour later, her answering machine was blinking. Automatically she hit the replay button and headed toward her purse that held Mr. Woodrow's phone number. The message stopped her.

"Hannah," the voice said, "call me at once. It's Sim – "

The voice went dead.

A moment later the machine once more kicked in.

"Hannah, it's Simona again. You know how I hate these mechanical things." She sighed audibly. "It cut me off before I finished my message. You can reach me on my cell. You've got the number and yes, I'll leave it turned on, I promise. Now be a dear and call me as soon as you get this message."

Hannah stared at the phone. Simona never used the answering machine. She viewed it with the same disdain she held for all things technical. Once before she had tried to leave a message but eventually had abandoned it, evidently unable to navigate the technology. The next day she told Hannah not to expect messages from her because she simply wouldn't use the machine again. Ever. Well, whatever she wanted must be important because not only had she used the answering machine but she had turned on her cell phone as well.

Without hesitation, Hannah called her.

The phone rang once.

"Thank goodness," Simona breathed into the phone. "Listen, dear, you simply must handle this for me."

"I'll do my best," Hannah told her. "What, exactly, do you want me to handle?"

"Why the bank, of course. It's Larry. Larry Woodrow. I like him and all that, but he can be such a stickler for protocol. He's holding my funds hostage. Hannah, you simply have to do something. The money's mine after all and I would think I could do with it as I choose."

"You're talking about the authorization for your bank draft?"

"Yes, whatever. I wrote a check and he refuses to cash it. You need to handle this for me."

"Simona, I can't authorize this kind of

transaction."

"No?"

To Hannah she sounded desperate.

"Well, then Jesher can. Tell him I need it done right away."

Hannah sank onto a chair. "It won't be that easy, Simona," she said. "Your son's a hard man to locate. I have already tried his office. He's unavailable."

"That's ridiculous. He's available, he just told his secretary to say that."

The pitch of Simona's voice was rising. She was fast becoming agitated.

"Call him on his cell, dear, just do it. Wait, I'll give you the number."

Hannah found a pen and jotted down the number as Simona spoke.

"This is important, Hannah. I refuse to be hogtied by the likes of Larry Woodrow. You tell Jesher I said so."

Hannah heard a series of tones while Simona hit number buttons as she tried to disconnect. A moment later all was quiet. Hannah let out a long sigh. She would never find Jesher if he didn't want to be found. Still, this was part of her job.

Ten minutes later Hannah was once again speaking with Simona. "If he's at work, Ms. McGuire won't put me through and I tried the number you gave me. He isn't picking up and neither is his voicemail. He's totally unplugged."

"Which means he's home. Go to his house. This

has to be settled."

"I can't do that," Hannah.

"Of course you can. If he's not at the office, that's where you'll find him. He does most of his work at home. Hannah, you find him and get this mess straightened out. Please. Alistair isn't going to be here much longer." She fumbled with the buttons again and finally disconnected.

Hannah's mood was glum. She doubted she would be able to resolve the situation at the bank because she wouldn't be able to locate Jesher. And she knew Simona was counting on her.

She picked up her car keys and headed out the door.

From a quarter of a mile down the road, Jesher saw a small black car void of any defining embellishment pull into his driveway. It shuddered slightly as the motor cut off. Then the driver popped the door and Hannah Swift stepped from the vehicle.

Jesher stopped his run to watch her. She walked differently today. The crisp business air that she wore like a plating of armor had dissolved. Her gait was soft and smooth and flowing. Her hair was free. It swirled about her head, defining the pattern of the breeze itself and giving her an earthy appeal that tore at his senses. A fierce, pagan response ripped through his body and he looked away. But he couldn't stay away. There was something compelling about this small woman who had entered his life.

The last leg of his run now abandoned, Jesher

stood entranced while sweat gathered in his thick hair and sluiced down his cheek and neck to form dark patches on his grey T-shirt. He headed toward his front door and the unexpected guest who stood nearby, intent on learning what brought her to his home.

"Hannah," he said when he was within earshot.

She swung toward him, cheeks darkened by surprise. He was always taller than she remembered him. And more striking. Always. He wiped the gathering moisture from his face with his sleeve. Immediately it returned. This time he took the tail of his shirt to stem the steady flow of sweat and in so doing revealed a hard abdomen darkened by the Caribbean sun. Hannah lowered her eyes, embarrassed to have unintentionally seen so much of the man who employed her.

"What brings you here?" he asked, forcing her eyes back to his face.

"Something has come up," she said. "It seems important to your mother. Actually she insisted I come to your home," she went on. She expected anger, or at least mild annoyance at having invaded his private turf.

Jesher gave his head a single, almost imperceptible shake and reached just inside the waistband of his running shorts to a pocket that held his house key. He stepped past her and unlocked the door.

"Come in." He motioned her into his home. "Mother isn't long in the patience department. What does she need this time?"

"Money," Hannah answered. Before she could say more, Jesher made his way through the sun-drenched living room of the stately home and returned a moment later with two bottles of water. He screwed the tops off both and handed one to Hannah. Then he motioned Hannah into a chair and collapsed in one that faced hers.

"Money?" he repeated. "Not possible. She couldn't spend all of hers in two lifetimes."

His nylon running shorts rode high on his thigh revealing skin the sun never saw. He seemed not to notice but it made Hannah blush.

"Especially if she can't access it," Hannah returned. She picked at the label on her water bottle and forced her attention back on topic.

"Especially then," Jesher said. "I take it the bank cut her off." His lips parted in a light smile.

Hannah nodded.

"What does she want to do this time? Take a trip?"

"She didn't say. By intent, I'd wager. The check's made out to cash." Hannah thought she heard him swear softly but she wasn't certain. "She needs you to make it right. She was quite insistent."

"I'll just bet she was." Jesher stood. The half split shorts he wore closed softly about his long, lean thighs. "I'll handle it," he said and a moment later she was alone.

Hannah was uncertain about the protocol to follow. Should she leave, business accomplished? This was, after all, her employer's home. That was the problem with Jesher. She was never sure how she stood with him, not really. She took a sip of her water and glanced around the place he called home.

The living room had been purposely divided into conversation groups that took the edge off the immensity of the space. The several sofas and club chairs were covered in leather and beneath each of the groupings lay an antique Heriz rug in shades of rust and bronze and navy. Though the masculinity of the furnishings suited their owner, Hannah had the clear notion that he'd had very little hand in selecting what now occupied his living space. He had undoubtedly handed off the task of making his home presentable to a decorator. And she would also guess that he had offered almost no direction.

Hannah pitied the woman, or man, who had had to deal with the likes of Jesher Kenyon and his house. She could imagine the unreturned phone calls, the requests for go-aheads on furniture orders and drapery selections that lacked replies. Despite what must surely have been an exasperating experience, the decorator had managed to pull together an unwieldy room with a flavor surprisingly reminiscent of its owner.

It was almost ten minutes before Jesher returned. In his absence he had removed his damp gray T-shirt and doused his head with water. Muscles flexed and bunched across his chest and shoulders as he toweled the excess moisture from his thick, wet hair.

"Done," he said and reaching for his water, finished it in a single swig. "That should make mother happy. Woodrow's a cautious man, but it is Mother's money to do with as she pleases." He took a step toward Hannah and quite suddenly there was no place for her to go.

She could feel the heat of him burning toward her, but it was the look in those green eyes of his that was setting her on fire. She knew what he intended and she wanted it more than she was willing to admit. She saw him lift his hands toward her face and she closed her eyes for his touch.

It never came.

Jesher paused his hands before dropping them once again to his sides. He was high from the run, intoxicated on endorphins that bathed his brain. Intoxicated by the small woman who had come to his door. Since the night of the Gala, whenever he thought of her – and the thoughts came with alarming frequency – he found himself aroused with an ease he had never known. He found himself consumed with thoughts of seeing her, of touching her, of loving her. He knew how she would look, her body bared by his hand. Her smooth tawny skin would be soft to his touch, her dark nipples rigid against his hungry mouth. He knew how she would feel, her body wet and tight around his swollen manhood, pulling at him, tugging him deeper inside her until, unable to hold back, he would explode within her.

Before he knew Hannah, such thoughts had not

been his daily fare. Sex, for him, was simple pleasure-taking, a physical release of short duration but easy enough to obtain as often as he needed it. Or wanted it.

Now it was different.

Now he found his usually centered mind adrift in scenes of flesh and heat and endless passion. All with Hannah. Only with Hannah. And those scenes left him in the company of frequent cold showers. It frustrated his fine sense of control. It disturbed him that a woman such as Hannah Swift could have such an effect on him.

He took his women with more sophistication and less determination than Hannah Swift. He took them cool and detached and uninvolved. All of which disturbed him even more because Hannah was no one he should want.

Except he did.

Desperately.

"Hannah Swift," he said, his voice barely above a whisper. "I don't know what to do with you."

Her cool opalescent eyes fluttered open.

"I should be working, but right now the only thing on my mind is this." He brushed his lips across hers in a tease that was barely a touch.

And he heard her sigh.

His long fingers reached out, gathering strands of her wonderful curling hair into his palm. He let it drift over the tips of his fingers in release, sensing its texture. Then he lowered his head and let his tongue play against the edges of her lips. He sipped at her, tasted her, breathed in the delicate scent of her.

Through the sheer fabric of her blouse Hannah felt the heat of him burning into her. Again he brushed his lips across hers. And once again. But his mouth was gone so soon that she had no time to respond. Today, it seemed, he intended to tease her, maybe to prove to them both that he could manage his passion with the same precision that he managed his everyday affairs.

"You smell like the morning," he said and caught the edge of her lower lip between his teeth.

Hannah moaned. He was seducing her and she knew it and she was powerless to stop him. She was hearing what he had probably told countless dozens of other women, feeling what they must have also felt. But even knowing that didn't change the fact that she desperately wanted him to kiss her deeply.

She reached her arms around his neck and drew him to her and just before he took her mouth, she felt his lips draw back in a smile.

And then the wanting and the waiting were over. His mouth was hotly against hers, his clever tongue insistent as it edged apart her lips and danced across the warm recesses of her mouth.

Jesher felt the tension that had been slowly mounting explode, felt the heat pool between his thighs. He was vaguely aware that he was wearing only nylon running shorts, cut for speed, not for love. Then the common sense and practicality of his daily life fled his passion-drenched brain and left him the puppet of his raging hormones.

He shuddered deeply, found her mouth again and wrapping his arms around her crushed her against him, mindless of his rapidly thickening manhood.

Against her stomach Hannah felt his thrust, hard and insistent pressing at her with primitive urgency. She felt the swirl of his mouth against hers, the dance of his tongue on hers. And then somewhere deep within her she felt the slippery moisture gather to ready her for his body.

When he finally lifted his head they were both breathing like a pair of spent racehorses. With his tongue he caught the moisture at the edges of her mouth. He lowered his palm to the sheer sunny colored linen of her blouse and drifted his fingers across the skin of her throat.

Her breath caught.

"I won't," he breathed into her hair, "do anything you don't want me to do."

His voice soothed. His voice made touching her all right, and Hannah gave up her caution. His fingers slipped inside the yellow fabric and then just beneath the lace edging of her bra, so quietly, so naturally that she never thought to tell him that what he wanted from her would never work.

Days later she was left to wonder where he would have taken her.

The ringing phone jarred her back to reality. Jesher drew the tip of his tongue across her ear lobe. "Forget it," he whispered when she drew away from him slightly. "The machine will pick up."

A moment later the ringing ceased and the crisp voice of Ms. McGuire filled the sunny living room. "Mr. Kenyon," she began, "there is a matter that needs your attention."

Jesher groaned. "This better not be Woodrow again," he said.

"Ms. Swift phoned in this afternoon with a request to you," the voice on the answering machine went on.

"Really?" Jesher murmured and took another nibble at Hannah's ear. "What request would that be, Ms. Swift?"

A fine shiver skittered across Hannah's shoulder blades. She inclined her head in a vain attempt to fend him off.

"She would like," Ms. McGuire continued, "a letter of reference from you. Evidently she has decided to seek employment elsewhere."

Jesher stopped feasting on his prize and straightened away from Hannah. He gave his head a solitary shake.

"Ordinarily," the secretary's voice continued, "this would not pose a problem. I have your standard letter on hand and can make the necessary adjustments. However, there was virtually nothing in her dossier, so I decided to make some inquires into her service at the Phipps Gallery." She paused for a breath and Hannah could imagine her tugging at her business suit with one hand while she adjusted her glasses with the other. "I discovered," she went on a moment later, "some information I think you should know."

Hannah stiffened.

"It is," Ms. McGuire continued, "regarding a certain Maxfield Parrish on loan from the Pennsylvania Academy of the Fine Arts. It seems that it disappeared on her watch."

CHAPTER SEVEN

Nothing about Jesher's half sister Lily looked like a Kenyon, except, of course, her height. Her skin was pale, her hair golden blond and her eyes the color of café au lait. Alistair might lay claim to her, but her genes must have belonged to her mother.

At the garden tea table Hannah watched the interplay of kin. Superficially, of course, everyone was polite. To be otherwise would have been unthinkable. Yet there were undercurrents of disdain so slight they could be missed entirely by the casual observer who might mistake the late afternoon scene for one of a congenial family gathering.

Hannah knew better.

In the library just beyond, Jesher paced, cell phone clamped to his ear. He had evidently come across a minor marble work by George Minne and was hoping for a quick sale.

"The Blochet," Simona was saying, "belonged to my great grandfather, Richard Woolley. That would be from the Poole side of the family, dear," she added a moment later and patted Lily's hand.

Alistair reached to the center of the table for a large pitcher of iced tea. He filled everyone's glass and then passed a small tray of sugar and lemon. Lily seemed genuinely interested in the story and Hannah wondered that she hadn't heard it before, having spent the better part of her youth living at Pinehurst. Or maybe she was just being polite.

"Great grandfather Woolley was no archaeologist, mind you," Simona went on. "He was an art dealer, and quite a clever one I've been told." Simona settled back into her chair. "There are two versions of how he came to own the Blochet. Both involve Kenneth Powell. Now Kenneth Powell was the sort who hung at the fringes of the archaeological digs with a fist full of American cash, seeking to buy treasure." She took a sip of her iced tea. "You must remember that in those days archaeologists were like treasure hunters. They frequently kept what they found. Or sold it to the highest bidder."

"So your great grandfather bought the Blochet?" Lily said.

Simona shook her head. "Not that he wouldn't have, given the opportunity, but, so the story goes, he had left the site when Pierre Blochet unearthed a series of limestone heads."

Hannah felt the back of her neck prickle and looked up to see Jesher leaning casually against the French doors that opened onto the patio where the family was seated. The nonchalance of his black T-shirt and well-worn blue jeans paid no attention to the serious expression he wore. The sale of the Minne, she would wager, had just gone sideways and Jesher Kenyon was not pleased.

"Pierre Blochet," Simona was saying, "was confounded by one of the three reserve heads he had discovered – the one now in my possession. You see, it was that of a common man, not a man of noble birth. A servant perhaps, or a farmer. And it seemed, at the time, an artifact of minor importance. His supplies were running low and he needed to pay his diggers. He remembered the dollars Powell had flashed about, contacted him and they struck a deal."

Alistair held out a glass of iced tea to his son who took it without comment and returned to the edge of the patio. Jesher swallowed a long gulp of the drink and drove his fingers through his hair. Then he snapped off his glasses and laid them carelessly on the ornate cast iron table to his left.

"Powell fetched it and immediately contacted my great grandfather so he could boast of his latest acquisition," Simona was saying. She made brief eye contact with everyone present, evidently reveling in her small but attentive audience. "Of course," she went on, "Grandfather Woolley wanted the Blochet, but he couldn't let on that he did. So he talked it down, said that it was worthless because it was the head of a common man. In effect," Simona said, smiling, "he undermined Powell's confidence, made him think he had been scammed."

"So you see, Lily," Jesher put in, "Grandfather Woolley and Kenneth Powell deserved each others' friendship. They were both just barely honest."

Lily looked up at her half brother and smiled.

"Then Grandfather offered Powell a deal." Simona said. "He had a charcoal detail from a lesser known work by Diego Velazquez that he offered in trade. Truth to tell, Grandfather had never really cared for the charcoal. In fact, the piece's attribution has never been substantiated." She turned to her son. "Still, it is an attractive work, don't you agree, Jesher?"

Jesher had moved back onto the patio, taking a chair between Alistair and Hannah. Beside her Hannah could feel his heat surging toward her, enveloping her as surely as his arms had a few days before. He spread his long legs out before him and crossed his ankles.

"It has good balance," Jesher returned. Then he reached out and draped an arm across the back of Hannah's chair in an absently casual gesture.

Hannah felt color rise to her cheeks.

"I would love to have seen the look on his face when he found out that this particular reserve head was more valuable than the others," Jesher added. He reached for his glass of iced tea and in so doing his arm slipped from the back of Hannah's chair to her shoulders. He seemed not to notice.

Hannah barely breathed.

"Kenneth Powell whined for a time," Simona went on, "but the deal for the Velazquez had already been struck. When his whining came to no good end, he threatened to come for the Blochet in the dead of night. Powell was a big man and I suspect he may have frightened Grandfather, what with his threats and all."

Jesher's hand found the soft, smooth skin of Hannah's upper arm, exposed on this warm afternoon by a cotton tank top. He drew the tip of his fingers across her flesh and when she didn't seem to mind, he did it again. He found the feel of her soothing, her softness delicious. He imagined drawing the tips of his fingers across the swell of her breasts and watching the darkened tips pucker in response to his touch. His body began to tighten and swell, filling the narrow space his jeans offered, and he tried to blink away the image he had composed of lying between her legs. Sweet Jesus but he wanted her.

"In the end," Simona was saying, "Powell's greatest revenge was the paranoia he evoked in my great grandfather. For the rest of his life, Richard Woolley kept the Blochet hidden away in his home. And the rest of us have kept up the family tradition of privacy. With the exception of the few scholars Grandfather allowed to view it, the Blochet has been publicly known only through photos."

"Until now," Lily said.

Simona nodded.

"Actually, Lily," Jesher said, "Grandfather Woolley did more than just hide the Blochet away. He had a clause added to his will, which extends to the fourth generation. It strictly forbids the selling of the Blochet and several other Egyptian artifacts he acquired under similar circumstances." Jesher had gone to drawing small circles on Hannah's arm with his forefinger. His touch made her shiver. And her shiver made him smile.

Simona looked again at her audience. "I said there were two versions. The other story is far more interesting."

"Only because it makes Grandfather Woolley more

of a rogue," Jesher said.

Simona waved her son quiet. "It starts the same way as the first, but in this story, instead of trading a Velazquez for the Blochet, Grandfather Woolley simply stole it from Powell." She drew a sliver of her ebony hair behind one ear. "We'll probably never know the truth and, of course, it doesn't matter after all. The Blochet is Poole property and will remain so. Grandfather saw to that."

"This sounds like some family feud," Lily said. "The Pooles and the Powells."

"Not at all," Simona said. "The dust is well settled. Now we just poke good-naturedly at each other. Why Malcolm is practically a member of the family."

"Malcolm?" Hannah said. She sat forward in her chair, and in so doing lost Jesher's touch.

"A nephew in the Powell family," Jesher said, "several generations removed, but the only living relative, just the same."

"And the charcoal hanging above the love seat in his living room?"

"Is the Velazquez," Jesher replied.

"Then if he has the charcoal," Hannah said, "it seems likely that your great grandfather did make the trade."

"You'd think so, wouldn't you?" Jesher offered. "But Malcolm has his own story." He shrugged. "It doesn't really matter any more. Like Mother said, the arguing between families has long since stopped."

The iced tea, the family stories all had been

interesting, but Hannah knew that wasn't why she was there. There was the matter of the Parrish and the exhibit at the Phipps Gallery. And Jesher wanted answers. He poured them each another iced tea and, taking her lightly by the elbow, led her into the family library.

Behind Hannah the French doors swung shut.

"I know what you're thinking," Hannah said when they were alone.

"Unlikely," Jesher replied. He had thought of little else but Hannah Swift since she had walked into his office to tell him the Blochet at the Royal Victoria Museum was a fake. He had thought about how she would look as he undressed her, how she would taste, how her eyes would flicker shut as his mouth found all her secret places. He had also thought about how empty his life would seem without her. She was unlike any woman he had ever met.

"I didn't do anything with that Maxfield Parrish. It was just misplaced. The courier from the Pennsylvania Academy was in a rush and picked up the wrong container. It happens."

Jesher set down his glass on an ancient lacquered Chinese chest and closed the space between them.

"The painting was recovered in Hanover, New Hampshire, at the Hood Museum." She stopped talking and looked squarely at Jesher. "But you already knew that, didn't you?"

"I told my secretary to hold off on the letter."

"Jesher, I want this position. Without the letter, I

don't stand a chance."

"We have unfinished business, you and I," he told her.

"The Blochet."

"Among other things," he said.

He was standing very close to her. The shadow of a beard darkened his face, making him look fearsome. Rough and untouchable. Maybe that's how other people saw him. Maybe that's what he wanted people to believe. But Hannah knew differently.

He inclined his head, but instead of kissing her, he found her ear, there to whisper dark things to her. His language was street coarse and graphic. He told her how she made him feel and how he would make her feel. He told her what he would do to her and what she could do to him.

And Hannah wanted him badly.

Behind them, the French doors opened. Late afternoon sun poured into the library, throwing Lily into silhouette. Hannah cleared her throat. Jesher levered away from her and jammed his hands into his pockets, hiding his erection.

"Sorry to bother," Lily said, "but I have information you need to know. There's been some unusual activity with your mother's account."

Lily refrained from actually calling Simona anything. Simona certainly was not her mother, though she had raised her. And maybe for that very reason, Lily felt equally uncomfortable calling Simona by her given name. So, instead, she called her nothing, a subtlety of unbearable significance.

Lily seated herself at the edge of a deep, leather club chair, her ankles crossed, her hands resting quietly in her lap. Her face wore a pleasantly serious expression. Working at a bank, if indeed she had to work at all, seemed an apt match for someone of Lily's demeanor.

Jesher turned away from Hannah. "It's been handled, Lily," he said. "Both Hannah and I have discussed the matter with Woodrow. I'm glad you're keeping an eye on things, though. We need an army to keep track of Mother."

Lily smiled in her benign way. To Hannah she seemed not so much at peace as done in. It was as if the world and its weight had already claimed her. "I doubt," she said softly, "that Mr. Woodrow knows about this." She looked straight at her half brother. "Frankly he would have no reason to check."

Before Jesher had the chance to respond, his cell phone rang. He reached into his pocket and started talking even as he walked away from the two women.

Hannah watched as he crossed the room. His stride was easy. Rangy. Despite his size he seemed confident, comfortable with the man he was.

Lily shifted in her chair. "He's a striking man, my brother," she said when Jesher was well away.

Hannah smiled. "Yes, he is."

"Doesn't date much, though." She allowed her eyes first to catch and then pin Hannah where she sat.

Hannah felt the intended stare and looked away.

"The occasional blonde," Lily was saying, "when he requires someone on his arm for a formal occasion. Or," she added more quietly, "to sate a need. They mean nothing to him, though."

Hannah sensed Lily meant to offer no conversational thread, so she only nodded.

"He's been around the block a time or two," Lily said.

Lily's choice of words caught Hannah by surprise and she played them again in her head. This was not the phrasing of those meticulously bred, of those who occupied the mansions east of the city. There was the occasional indelicacy to Lily's speech that slipped through the smooth and practiced patterns she had learned.

"And he's made some mistakes," Lily went on.

"Everyone does," Hannah returned.

"He was engaged, you know."

"I heard," Hannah replied, and wondered at the direction Lily was taking.

"Well, I guess the whole city heard," Lily said. Her voice turned sharp. "Savatheda never made any tries at hiding her affair." Her face brightened to a harsh shade of pink. "She publicly embarrassed Jesher."

"It was unfortunate." Hannah glanced past the young woman in search of Jesher. She wanted him back in the room to halt Lily's spreading tension.

"He won't make that mistake again, getting involved with a woman like that."

Hannah was saved from responding by Jesher's

return. He dropped his phone into his pocket and walked to the windows where he stood staring at the gardens beyond. His silence, Hannah suspected, was precipitated by whatever had just transpired over the phone.

"Jesher," Lily said quietly, "we need to finish talking about the situation at the bank."

For a moment he didn't respond, then he turned slowly back to his sister. His eyes were distant, his attention gone.

"Jesher?" Lily said.

He took the club chair next to Hannah and focused on his sister. "So," he said when he was well settled in, "what do I need to know about Mother?"

"There was a large deposit made to her checking account," Lily said flatly.

"And then she drew it out. I told you I handled it," Jesher returned and stood. "It's mother's money to do with as she pleases."

"I understand that," Lily returned. "But aren't you the least curious about where that money came from?"

"Not particularly," Jesher said. "She cashed in some bonds, sold some stocks. It doesn't matter." He walked to Hannah's chair and held out a hand, a signal for her to stand.

Lily shook her head. "I ran a check on her holdings. The accounts, at least the ones I have access to, have been systematically emptied."

Before Jesher could respond, his cell phone rang again. He checked the caller I.D. and dropped it back into his pocket, unanswered. "You shouldn't do that," he said to Lily. "Spy on her accounts."

Lily smiled.

Jesher lofted an eyebrow. "I don't want to know. Besides, it's mother's money, not mine. She can do whatever she wants with it."

"Including giving fistsful of it to our father?"

* * *

Jesher followed Hannah out the front door of Pinehurst. He had never answered Lily, leaving Hannah to wonder if he didn't care or if he was too angry to speak.

"Are you hungry?" he said when she had turned to tell him goodbye.

"Starved," she returned.

"Good. I like women with a healthy appetite." He jangled his car keys in front of her. "Restaurant or take-out?"

"Take-out," she told him."

Moments later they were heading across town. Hannah watched the muscles in Jesher's jaw flex and his grip tighten down on the leather steering wheel. The children of Alistair Kenyon were intense for sure, though she wondered where such steady seriousness had its roots. Certainly not in their father.

"Lily is very protective of you," Hannah said.

"Is that what she told you?"

"Pretty much. She wrapped her warning in a story

but I got the message."

Jesher shook his head. "I never could get Lily to lighten up. She doesn't smile, she never did. And she doesn't handle change well either. It was hard on her when Dad left. I guess she thinks I'm all she has left, now."

"What about your mother?"

Jesher shrugged. "They're civil. Beyond that I don't know. Lily goes her way and I go mine, except for the occasional must-show at Pinehurst." He pulled the car to a stop in front of Sinbad's Restaurant. "Mediterranean OK with you?"

Hannah nodded. "Anything as long as it's food."

"Good," he returned. "I haven't had any falafel in a long time. It's a weakness I acquired overseas and this place does it right. I know the owner."

An hour later they were seated in Hannah's living room, paper containers covering the surface of an old caisson seat Hannah used as a coffee table. Beside it Hannah knelt, dishing out dinner. While the cottage had a dining room, it had no furniture. And the kitchen was a functional place meant only for meal preparation.

Jesher watched while Hannah constructed an enormous pita pocket and then deftly cut the whole affair in half. In his thirty-seven years he had never known anyone like her. She was bright and she was unpretentious. And she possessed an innate sensuality she would deny in a furious blush if he told her. Nevertheless there it was, in the way she held herself, in the way she walked. And especially in the way she traveled her eyes over him. It left him as tight as a fourteen-year-old boy who had just been allowed the pleasure of unfastening his first bra.

Hannah reached across the pitted surface of the wagon seat for the tahini sauce, drizzled it over the cut pockets of bread and offered him one half. Instead of taking the food, Jesher took her lightly by the wrist, leaned forward and lowering his lips, licked away the yoghurt and sesame concoction that had dripped there. He heard Hannah's breath catch at the light touch of his tongue and he smiled. It was as though she had never known sensual pleasure before. She was tinder waiting for his match.

He wondered if she knew.

He released her wrist and reached for the bottle of chardonnay. "Good choice," he said.

Hannah shrugged, then took a seat beside him. She nested herself cozily into the corner of her sofa, curling her legs beneath her. "I don't know much about wines, but I know what I like."

"Then you have a natural gift."

Hannah caught the edge of his gaze. It was intense. Jesher never seemed to let down his guard. It was the business, she would wager, that kept him on his toes. The next phone call, the next fax could seal the deal of a lifetime.

Jesher's cell phone rang and he reached into his pocket to silence it.

"Aren't you going to take that?" Hannah said.

He slid his forefingers behind his glasses and rubbed his eyes. "It can wait."

Hannah looked up, surprised. She thought his business fed his soul.

"Collectors are a demanding bunch," he said. "They want the impossible and they want it yesterday because they're having a cocktail party tomorrow and some lesser member of a royal family has just decided to come after all." He took a sip of his wine. "It doesn't stop."

"Do you?"

He frowned before he spoke. "I try."

"How do you stop?"

"Run. I run. Anywhere I can, as often as I can." And the same narcotic that drenched his brain at the end of a run now taunted him with notions of lying with Hannah. He forced his eyes to focus on the wall just beyond her face.

"What else?"

In spite of himself, Jesher looked back at Hannah, taking her on with his soft, green gaze. "Nothing else."

"Well, that's the problem right there. Running fires you up. You need to cool down, let everything go, free your mind."

"What do you do, Hannah, to set your mind free?"

"Pots," she answered simply.

Jesher laughed. "How sixties of you. My drug of choice is a good business deal."

"Not pot. Pots. I make pots. I throw clay on a wheel and touch it and watch it spin and shape it into simple, functional forms. I focus on the lump in front of me and everything else disappears." She took a piece of pita bread and dipped it into the tahini sauce. The smooth buttery flavor acted like its own narcotic. "You of all people," she went on after a moment, "should know the benefits of using your hands to free your mind. Look at your mother. Her life is sculpting."

"Simona has talent." He took off his glasses and, folding them, set them on the bench in front of him. Then he hooked a finger beneath her chin and tilted her head slightly. With almost no movement at all he could put his lips against hers and then he would be able to taste her again. Instead he sucked in a long breath and waited for the heat that was already tightening him to dissipate. "You're a regular little oracle, aren't you Hannah Swift?" he said when he thought he could trust himself. "You can fix my headaches and you can fix my career. You can even fix my leisure time." He inclined his head until he was a breath away from her, helpless to stop his desire to kiss her and knowing that she could also fix the heat that was burning through his veins.

"That sounded bossy," she said not daring to move even a hair's breadth or his mouth would be on hers, "when I didn't mean it to at all."

"I didn't take it that way," he returned and slipped the tip of his tongue across her pouty lower lip.

Her eyes fluttered shut while she took in the sensation.

"No one has ever offered me life lessons before.

Not Mother, she has always been in her own world. And certainly not Dad, given the state of his own life." He let his tongue slide across her upper lip this time and watched as she bathed shamelessly in the sensation. "You are wise beyond your years, Hannah Swift."

Hannah forced her eyes open and found he had returned to his own space. Disappointment twinged her stomach. "I have a younger brother, so I guess preachiness goes with the birth order." He might have moved away but the heat was still there in his cool green gaze. She knew he wanted her. She just wasn't sure what he planned to do about it. She leaned forward to gather up the shards of their meal and felt his hand lightly on her shoulder.

"In a minute," he said. Then his cell phone rang and he flicked it silent a second time.

"You've got work to do," she told him, "calls to return."

"Nothing important."

His voice had gone husky on her, crackling with the words, barely breaking a whisper. It gave her chills. Ignoring his request, she leaned forward, picked up a handful of containers and whisked them off the surface of the ancient seat. Then she stood and started toward the kitchen. "I don't like messes," she said lightly. When he didn't respond, she knew her decision to break off the moment had been the right one.

She dumped the containers into the garbage can

and when she did so, the leftover tahini sauce splashed up, speckling her hands and cheek before settling on the front of her pale linen blouse. She groaned in disgust, pulled off a piece of paper towel and wet it. Then she daubed away at the sauce, hoping it would leave no permanent record of her clumsiness.

"I'd be happy to give you a hand with that."

Hannah swung around and found Jesher altogether too close. Without waiting for a reply he lifted the dampened towel from her fingers and with precise care dabbed at one of the several spots she had not yet tried to clean.

Hannah shut her eyes and swallowed. He wasn't doing anything, not really. Just trying to help her clean herself up. And there was certainly nothing intentionally sensuous about the way he was going about it. At least she didn't think there was. One of his hands rested lightly on her shoulder, for balance probably, while with the other he gently blotted the pink linen fabric of her blouse. Still, where he touched her, she burned.

She felt an angry blush rise and tried to fight it down. But if Jesher saw it, and surely he did, he gave no indication. Instead he meticulously and methodically worked at her stain with the cheery red and white and yellow paper towel, his gaze intent on the task at hand.

The kitchen air grew palpably tense.

He was close enough that Hannah could catch the fresh scent of his soap, pine and something else she couldn't name. He was close enough that she could see the slow and gentle rise and fall of his chest as he breathed. Everywhere she looked there was Jesher, his dark hair tumbling over his forehead, his chest a wall of black fabric, his clever fingers stroking her as if there were no fabric to cover her at all.

When she could bear no more, she cleared her throat. "I'm sure that's got it. Thanks for your help." She chanced a look at him, hoping his expression was as neutral as his behavior had been.

He stepped, or maybe only leaned, away from her slightly and passed his eyes quickly over her face once and then again before devouring her slowly, inch by inch. Hannah's breath quickened. She looked away only to see her breasts moving against the dampened tissue thin fabric that now clung to her flesh. Her eyes moved from the sight of her visibly pounding heart to a smile that lilted across Jesher's lips. He was enjoying the effect he was having on her and the notion raised her blood indignantly. "Thanks again for dinner," she said. "The falafel was great. I can see why you like it so much," she added and started around him.

Although she hadn't actually seen him move, suddenly there he was, again in front of her, quietly blocking her way. Before she could either protest or move, he lowered his head and lightly took her mouth. Tonight she was pliant in his arms, just as she always was, her flesh willing even though her words said otherwise. Jesher felt her body sigh against his and reveled in the sensation. He closed his arms around her, drawing her into him and she offered no resistance.

And like molten lava, he felt heat surge through his veins. If he had thought at all, he would have known that in a matter of moments it would require a herculean effort to wrest control from the hormones that were flooding his body. But he couldn't think. He could only respond to the small woman he held. And his response was dark and pagan and deeply sensuous. He lowered his head to the soft curve of her neck, there to linger kisses while he took in her scent, a delicate floral cologne mixed with something earthier, something headier. It tightened him unexpectedly.

Jesher was aware of the coos of pleasure drifting from her lips. He was also vaguely aware that they were still in her kitchen. But by now he was rock hard and ready, his erection pressing uncomfortably against the small pouch his jeans offered up.

"Christ I want you," he said.

In response, Hannah put her arms around his neck and in so doing slid her body along his in a seductive little shimmy. Jesher almost came undone. He had meant to seduce her, to woo her slowly and carefully so she would not deny him, deny them both. But it was too late for that now. His brain was drenched in the stuff of primitive urges and his body was responding despite his vague stabs at intellectual reasoning. He squeezed shut his eyes and gritted his teeth in one final effort to recapture control of his strangely errant body. And he had almost won the battle when Hannah made a little purring sound and moved her hips against his.

Without saying a word, he dropped his mouth to hers and while he drove his tongue inside her, he drove her body to the wall. He clawed at her blouse and then her bra until she was bare for him. Then he closed his mouth over her taut, dark flesh and drank her deeply. Beneath him she squirmed. She writhed. She moaned with sensual pleasure.

Somewhere in the reality that was her kitchen he heard her call his name and then she was grabbing for him, trying to find him, to touch him. He lifted her toward him.

"Wrap your legs around me," he told her and felt her settle against the hard shelf of his throbbing manhood.

Hannah's generously gored skirt fell away high at the thigh exposing lean, muscular legs all done up in smooth skin. Jesher sucked in a hard breath and started out of the cheery cherry kitchen to a bed somewhere, or, barring that, any horizontal surface where he could lay her down and plunge himself into her.

They made it as far as the opposite wall.

"Jesus," he muttered under his breath. He realized that he was going to come and there was nothing he could do to stave it off. He set her on the counter top and hooking a finger into the leg of her panties pulled them from her in a single movement. She was wet already and swollen with desire. His shaking hands fumbled with the buttons of his fly and a moment later his throbbing erection burst from its confinement.

He tugged her to the edge of the counter and there drove himself deeply into her. She was hot and tight around him and her flesh was already beginning its convulsing spiral into nothingness.

"Jesher," she whispered as he withdrew and drove into her again. Then he felt her come apart in his arms. She shuddered, she shook, she sighed all at once. And then she tightened down on him drawing him deeper within her with each successive wave of her climax. He ground at his teeth wanting to stave off his moment of pleasure but she squeezed him again and thrusting deeply one final time, he spilled himself relentlessly into her.

CHAPTER EIGHT

"You've really outdone yourself this time." Hannah's own worried face stared back at her from the bathroom mirror. She shook her head in disgust and yanked the brush through her morning tangle of curls.

"On the kitchen counter," she added aloud. Then she tossed the brush into a basket on the toilet tank and wondered how she would ever be able to face Jesher.

Ten minutes later she stepped from the shower, certain that, given the most recent circumstances, she needed to move on. The position at the Ashfield Gallery wouldn't be available for very long. So, she would remind Jesher that nothing untoward had actually happened to the Maxfield Parrish painting. She would remind him that the painting had, in fact, been recovered. And then she would ask him again for a letter of recommendation.

She padded back into her bedroom and was almost dressed when she noticed a voicemail on her phone. She hit the message button and then speaker. A moment later she heard Turner's voice.

"Hannah, if you're there, pick up." He paused. "I mean it, this is serious."

The machine clicked off.

Hannah frowned at her phone and had started to button her blouse when she heard Turner's voice again.

"OK, Sis, listen up," Turner's voicemail said. "You

124

and me, we could be in some really deep shit. I met a guy who knows some stuff, stuff about those pieces we took to Toronto. If this dude's got the song right, . . . Christ, Hannah why can't you just be there when I need you?"

The phone went dead.

Hannah stared bleakly at her reflection in the bedroom mirror, wondering at the mess she had just created in her life and wondering what mess awaited her in her brother's very private world. She pressed redial hoping to find out what Turner meant. No answer. Just to be thorough she dialed his landline, even though she doubted he would answer. He didn't.

Turner, it seemed was unplugged.

Hannah started toward the kitchen to make some coffee but paused at the doorway. Images of Jesher tore through her mind leaving her shaky, leaving her flushed. She squeezed shut her eyes against the assault of sights and sounds and smells that filled her, and wondered if she could ever sort through the recent events that had turned her life upside down.

Behind her the doorbell rang.

"I brought you coffee." Jesher stood at the threshold and held up a small paper bag. "And a muffin." He held up another bag.

Hannah unlatched the screen and stepped aside for him to enter.

"I've been thinking," he remarked casually and walked into her living room.

Hannah waited for his apology. And his following

request that they both put the events of the previous night away and promise never to retrieve them.

"There's something we need to do." He set the two paper bags carefully on Hannah's coffee table and disappeared into the kitchen. A moment later he returned carrying two plates, a knife and some napkins.

Hannah sank onto the sofa and braced herself for the inevitable. He was sorry, he would tell her, that he had let things get out of hand. It wasn't like him, he would say, and then he would let her know in no uncertain terms that what had happened in her kitchen meant nothing.

Hannah wished herself in another country.

"We've got to see Mother's copy of the Blochet for ourselves," he told her instead. Then he settled himself next to Hannah, opened one bag and handed her a thick paper cup.

Hannah took off the plastic lid and let the aroma engulf her. He had brought her coffee made from a Costa Rican grind, her favorite. She smiled in spite of her dismal mood.

"I convinced the counter man at *C'est Si Bon* to brew up a pot. Hope you like it." Then he opened the second bag and pulled out two muffins. "Cranberry or poppy seed?"

"You pick," she said and took another sip of her coffee. Its musky flavor soothed her frayed nerves.

Jesher cut the muffins in half and set the whole affair on the coffee table. He could guess Hannah was more than a little uncomfortable with his presence this morning, which was exactly why he had come. Feelings like that could fester if left alone and when things festered, they frequently became bigger. And uglier. He couldn't let that happen. He would force her to see him, to talk with him until she was again at ease in his company.

He aimed his conversation at neutral turf. "After we eat," he suggested rather blandly, "we should go up to the main house and ask Mother if we can see her copy of the Blochet."

But Hannah didn't think it was a good idea. "Remember how upset she was before when you asked about her copy?"

But Jesher wasn't buying Hannah's concern. "If Mother's copy is gone, then it's probably the one on display at the Vic."

"And that means someone who knew about the copy, someone close to your mother, may have taken it, doesn't it?"

Jesher shrugged. "First things first. Let's take a look at Mother's copy. My guess is she's locked it away in her vault." Jesher took up a piece of poppy seed muffin and held it out to Hannah who shook her head.

"Why would she lock away a study that she made herself?"

"My mother is a little protective of her art – all of it – as I'm sure you have noticed. Keep in mind that the Blochet itself has been held privately almost since its discovery." He took a bite out of the muffin then held it out for her again.

Again she shook him off.

"There are only a few images of it, and those are years old and grainy. If someone substituted Mother's copy for the original Blochet, almost no one would know."

Hannah took a sip of her coffee and leaned back against her sofa. "Except us."

"You should eat," Jesher said.

"I'm not hungry."

He popped the rest of the muffin into his mouth and washed it down with a healthy swig of coffee. "I see."

Hannah looked up at him and was met with an inscrutable expression. She set down her coffee cup, took a deep breath and plunged into the disaster she had helped create. "About last night," she began.

She felt his beautiful green eyes all over her and it made her blush. She had never blushed until Jesher. Then again, she had never had any reason to do so. Until Jesher. She gathered up her long hair, braided it loosely behind her neck and secured it with a small rubber band from around her wrist. She had made love with this man on her kitchen counter. Her face reddened with the very thought. "It was a mistake," she said at last. "I don't know what came over me."

"It wasn't a mistake," he told her and there for an instant he made her believe it was true. "We've both known this was coming for a long time."

128

"We have?" she said and looked at him squarely.

"We have."

"Speak for yourself," she told him.

Jesher chose not to answer, instead aimlessly stirring his half-filled coffee cup.

"How could I have known it was coming," Hannah went on. "We haven't ever even been on a date." It all sounded so antiquated when she actually said it. Did people really go on dates any more? Before they hooked up? She rolled her eyes and wished herself buried ten feet under. It wasn't that she hadn't enjoyed herself. But she simply didn't do such things.

Except she had.

"Is that a prerequisite," Jesher asked. "Going on a date?"

"Well I'd like to think there is some logical progression before people . . ." she stumbled over the words and fell silent..

"Make love?" Jesher offered neutrally.

"I don't want to talk about it."

He raised one thick, dark eyebrow. "Then have something to eat," he said after a moment. "You'll need your strength for Mother."

Ten minutes later they were in Simona's studio.

"Good morning, dear," Simona said. Her back was to the studio door and she was selecting some tools while a bucket in the sink filled with water. "I'm not pleased with the surface of *The Collector*. It's too rough." She pointed to the sink. "Jesher be a dear and turn off the water, won't you?"

Jesher wandered over to the spigot and flicked it off. Jeans hung loosely on his lean hips. The T-shirt tucked into them followed the muscles of his upper arms and shoulders like another skin. Hannah found herself in a heated flush and looked away.

"So I've decided to trowel on a finer grade of cement," Simona was saying. "The wheelbarrow's already at the site. I just need that water for cleaning my tools." She turned around and looked at her son. "If you don't mind."

Jesher picked up the bucket and carried it outside.

"It seems you two are getting along better," Simona said when Jesher was away from them. "I'm glad for that."

Hannah didn't know how to respond to the comment so she merely nodded.

Simona was dressed in her coveralls, her hair – today Rosy Russet– tied away from her face with a bandana. She picked up her tools and headed for the door. "You coming? It's been days since you've seen my lady."

Obediently Hannah followed the other woman to the site of her latest project. Jesher was waiting by the statue that stood nearly eight feet tall.

"I've had a devil of a time with her texture," Simona said as they approached. "I want it rough enough to hold moss, but I don't want it pocked. Here we are." She set down her tools, filled a pail with her latest batch of cement and started troweling it over the base of the statue.

Jesher indulged his mother's meandering chat only for a moment longer before requesting to see her copy of the Blochet.

"I've taken care of everything, dear," Simona said and filled a second pail with cement.

"Still," Jesher said quietly, "I need to check on some things."

Hannah marveled at the delicately indulgent approach Jesher took with his mother, sidestepping her oblique responses and moving ahead with his agenda.

"Well, it's safe. It's locked away and no one can get at it."

"In the vault?"

"Of course," Simona said.

"With your permission, I'd like to check."

"You don't believe me." Simona's voice sounded almost pouty.

"I do believe you, Mother. Unfortunately not everyone in the world is as completely honest as you."

Simona merely shrugged and then, turning her back on them both, headed up her stepladder to the shoulders of *The Collector of Life*.

* * *

The vault stood squarely in the middle of the main house. A 1960's addition, it was accessible only through a sliding panel in the dining room. Its interior was not as large as Hannah had expected, given the fact that it housed pieces of original artwork and not just the family gems. It was, in fact, forbiddingly confining.

Jesher found the overhead light which did nothing to dispel the eerie sensation crawling over Hannah. The steel paneled vault had the feel of a family mausoleum. Airtight, temperature controlled, and probably sound proof, this little room checked all the boxes for a horror movie. A shiver licked Hannah's shoulder blades.

"You coming?" Jesher said.

"I'll wait here," she told him.

Jesher gave her a shrug, then turned toward the vault and stepped inside. He pushed past several crates made for oil paintings, and moved several small boxes before spotting what appeared to be a draped piece of statuary near the rear of the room.

Hannah craned to see what he had found, but without actually following him into the vault she was unable to see.

"This is not what I hoped for," he said, a moment later. A cloth used to cover unfinished art dangled from one of his hands. Next to him was Simona's copy of *L'homme Ordinaire* – the Blochet. "Mother's study," he said. He motioned Hannah into the vault.

Hannah bent forward to see a copy of the limestone face of a man from the Fourth Egyptian Dynasty. A moment later she nodded. The edge of the upper lip and an area near the brow line both held tiny but unmistakable marks from the chisel that belonged to Simona Poole Kenyon.

"But we both saw similar imperfections on the head at the Vic," Hannah said. "I was sure it was Simona's."

Jesher didn't reply. Instead he took the cloth and draped it over the limestone copy.

"Could she have made more than one?" Hannah said.

Jesher nodded toward the door. "Let's ask her."

It was a last best hope and they both knew it. If the Blochet on view at the Vic was Simona's copy then the theft was likely contained. Only those who were close to Simona would even have known of the existence of such a copy. It occurred to Hannah that the copy might even have been shipped accidently, leaving the real Blochet safe and sound. Somewhere.

But, if the Blochet on view at the Vic wasn't Simona's copy, then the theft and its replacement were no longer limited to Simona's intimate circle. And the list of those potentially involved became immediately limitless. Hannah shivered remembering her brother's words. Somebody knew something about the pieces she and Turner had accompanied to Toronto. And whatever Turner had heard had shaken him badly. She knew she should tell Jesher about the message.

"Mother," Jesher said while still some distance from *The Collector of Life*.

Simona didn't answer.

It was peaceful in the woods beyond the main house, and quiet. And Simona seemed totally absorbed

133

in her work. She stood near the top rung of her ladder, troweling cement onto the shoulders and neck of her beloved statue.

Jesher stopped at the foot of a nearby pine and looked up. "Mother," he said again, "could you come down for a moment?"

"Really dear," she said without turning around to face her son. "I want to finish this project. Time is important."

"So is this. It will only take a moment. I need to talk to you and it's difficult if you're up there."

Simona gave an audible sigh, placed the trowel in her bucket and started backing down the ladder. "This couldn't wait?" she asked when she was back on the ground. She looked up at her son and blinked at his serious expression. "I guess not," she answered for herself. Then she walked around her son and looked up at him again. "You don't go to work dressed like that, do you?"

Jesher shook his head.

"Because you were raised better. You wear a proper suit and tie, yes? People won't take you seriously if you look like this." She closed her eyes and shook her head slowly.

Jesher raked back his hair and Hannah noticed a bit of color creeping up the sides of his neck.

"Mother, did you make more than one copy of the Blochet?"

Simona frowned for a moment. "As I told you," she said, "I couldn't get the mouth right. Mouths have always given me trouble. They're not as easy as one might think. Maybe that's why my *Collector* doesn't have a well-formed face. I decided just to give the illusion of expression. It works well, don't you think?"

"So, you made a study of the mouth and one complete copy of the head. Is that right?" Jesher said.

Simona frowned and leaned against the ladder. "No, just the one," Simona told him.

"One mouth? Or one entire head?"

Simona put her foot on the first rung of the ladder. Then she put it back on the ground and turned toward her son. "Did Eddie say something to you? Is that what this is all about?"

"Eddie? You mean Dr. Dewald?"

Simona nodded. "I told him it was just an idea. But he became so upset." She shook her head and frowned a bit.

Jesher walked up to his mother and put his arm around her small shoulders. "Mother," he said quietly, "you need to explain. Please. It's important."

Simona sighed audibly. "Well, you know that the Blochet belongs to the Poole side of the family. And you know," she went on, "that it has always stayed within the confines of Pinehurst."

Jesher nodded without pressing his mother.

Simona shrugged. "It was just an idea I had. I told Eddie that since no one had ever really seen the Blochet, maybe I would just send my copy to the Vic for the exhibit instead of sending the real thing."

To Jesher's credit he neither moved nor spoke.

135

"But, of course, Eddie wouldn't have it. He said he was curating the exhibit and he simply couldn't have a reproduction, copy, whatever," she gave her hand an upward flourish. "He said *Voices From The Past* was an important exhibit and it had to be authentic. Even though," she looked at first her son and then Hannah, "we know that copies are frequently used for such events."

"So you sent the real *L'homme Ordinaire* to Toronto?" Jesher said.

"Of course. I couldn't stand to see the look on Eddie's face."

"And put your copy in the vault?"

She looked up at her son. "As you said. Now Jesher, my cement will be too dry if I don't get back to work." A moment later a smile slowly broke on her face. When Hannah followed her line of sight she saw what had caught Simona's attention. Alistair was making his way from the main house to the clearing where *The Collector of Life* stood awaiting a final coat of cement.

"If there aren't any more questions, dear, I must get back to work. I need to finish *The Collector*. She will be my final effort and I want her to be perfect." She picked up her bucket of cement and her trowel and started back up the ladder. Half way to the top she stopped and turned. "I don't have much time left, you know."

CHAPTER NINE

"It could be months – years – before we find out what happened to the Blochet." Hannah sucked in an exasperated breath and leaned forward in her chair. She had come to Jesher's office by invitation. For lunch, he had said over the phone that morning. He would order in, he had said. But now they were embroiled in the same discussion that had driven them for the last several days.

"We might never find out," she said. "Jesher, I really need that letter of reference, or I won't get the job."

And he knew it.

"I'm sorry *L'homme Ordinaire* is gone," she went on after a moment, "especially for Simona's sake. I know she'll be upset and I hate that. But the fate of the Blochet is a Kenyon problem. And now that you know the theft has a broader scope than you thought, maybe you should involve the police and make it their problem as well."

Jesher shook her off. "Out of the question."

"So your plan is to keep me in your employ until you're satisfied that I had no part in this theft?" She took a moment to stare down the man who was single-handedly deciding her fate. "

"And Turner," Jesher told her.

"Turner? Good luck with that."

"I've offered him a job."

Hannah's head came up sharply. "Doing what?

He's not exactly an aficionado of fine art. In case you hadn't noticed."

"But he does know security." Jesher walked around his desk and sat. "He's got a good record of service."

"Except for his stint with AmRaq."

Jesher nodded. "Except for that."

"And he agreed to work for you?"

"I made him an offer he couldn't refuse."

Hannah had a bad feeling. Jesher and Turner were a lethal mix. Jesher's business was all about discretion and refinement. Finesse. And her brother didn't know the meaning of the word. Turner was confrontational and self-assured. Just like Jesher. It would only be a matter of days before one of them postured and dared the other to do something about it. "Mind if I ask what that offer was?"

Jesher shrugged. "I took care of his debt. Up front. He needs to work it off."

Hannah sank back onto the client chair. She had hoped to extricate herself from the business of the Blochet, the copy of the Blochet and the entire Kenyon family. Especially the Kenyons. Well, Jesher, at any rate. Because, despite how he made her feel, he was someone who could just never work out. He moved in higher circles than she did. He operated through phone calls and handshakes and gifted bottles of Nolet Reserve.

Space. That was what she needed between her and Jesher. A job in another city, or better yet, another

No Ordinary Man

state. But Jesher wasn't going to help her out. Worse, now he had involved her brother in the business of the Kenyon family.

"You can't be serious," she said after a moment.

"As a heart attack. I gave him what he needed to get out from under."

"Did you ask out from under what?"

"Not my business. He knows he has to honor the debt to me. I don't care about the details."

And there it was. That darker side of Jesher that left Hannah always feeling a little uneasy. Hannah drew in a long breath. "It sounds a little like blackmail to me," she told him.

"He jumped at the chance."

"The Blochet is gone. It's not some prank that one of Simona's student's played on her. And Turner and I didn't sneak it away. It's a real, live art theft. Keeping my brother and me close won't bring it home. Jesher, do yourself a favor. Do all of us a favor. Call the police."

Jesher took off his glasses, folded in their gold wire sidepieces and placed them on his desk. Then he allowed himself one long draught of Hannah Swift. He had thought to get her completely out of his system that night in her kitchen, but he had been wrong. He wanted her now more than ever. She drove his nights into sweats, the deep, restless kind he thought he had left with his youth. And she forced him into bone chilling showers well before dawn. "If the Blochet is on the street, " he said, "I'll know."

Hannah made an accusatory sniff and saw with more than a little satisfaction as he stiffened slightly at the noise. "So, no to the letter of reference?"

Jesher turned and allowed his cool green eyes to wash over her, but he didn't reply.

"I need to leave," Hannah said. She gathered up her purse, keys and jacket, and stood. "I find that I'm really not hungry."

"The disappearance of the Blochet is a serious loss," Jesher stated, his voice in a neutral place. "And I take it seriously." He walked behind his desk where, with a single keystroke, he brought his dozing computer screen to life.

If he said anything else, Hannah didn't know. She had already left his office.

* * *

Jesher leaned back in his chair and stared out his office window. Far below, the river flowed brown and angry as it bisected the city on its way to Lake Ontario. He took pride in his ability to make deals in the art world. He knew who wanted what and he knew what they would pay to have it. But recently his personal affairs had taken a hit.

There was, of course, the matter of the Blochet. If it had hit the open market, and he felt it had, he might well never see it again. The provenance of the piece was clear and well documented, a fact which made it all the more desirable. The statue would be a prize for anyone willing to pay the price. And there would be nothing he could do to stop it.

There was also the matter of Hannah Swift. From the day he met her, he had convinced himself that they had nothing in common, other than a love of fine art. And he had been able to relegate thoughts of her to a seldom-visited place in his mind. That is until this spring when he had asked her to accompany *L'homme Ordinaire* to the Royal Victoria Museum. He didn't know exactly what had changed, or how, or even when, but she was there, driven deep into his thoughts. And there she had stayed, unbidden. Unsettling him, leaving him feeling off balance.

Leaving him wanting.

He squeezed shut his eyes, remembering the feel of her soft skin, the fragrance of her hair, like herbs and honey. Thief or not, he wanted her again. Hell, he wanted her all the time. And he didn't know what he was going to do about it.

* * *

Hannah wove the small scratching noises seamlessly into her dream. Dumpling, her childhood cat was there by her chin as she slept, pawing at the covers until he could burrow beneath the blankets. Once there, he would wrap himself around her feet and purr contentedly.

Again came the noise, this time louder, forcing Hannah's eyes open. Blackness blanketed her bedroom. She rolled over and closing her eyes, re-entered a world where cats, long since gone, could warm her toes.

When the scratching persisted Hannah knew it was not her dream. For a time she lay still, paralyzed by fear only a city dweller could comprehend. An animal, a raccoon or worse, was trying to gain entry into the guest cottage she called home. Hannah appreciated wild life where it belonged. Outside. Only once had she encountered a creature from the wild in her home, a field mouse that had worked its way into her basement seeking warmth in an endless winter.

But here on an estate that occupied acres of wooded land, all manner of beasts roamed freely. And tonight, it seemed, one had decided to enter her domain. She waited, motionless on her bed, for the sound to come again.

Moments later it did.

This time it was louder.

Or nearer.

In the bed, Hannah shivered. Raccoons, she had heard, at least some of them, were rabid. She would be defenseless against such a crazed and drooling creature. She shivered again and reached for the phone beside her bed.

The next sound she heard stopped her even as she dialed the main house. Someone had whispered her name. So softly was it pronounced the first time, that Hannah was not certain she had really heard it. But it came again, and then she was sure. She set down the phone and strained against the endless black that had claimed her room. Darkness, thick and heavy, filled her eyes. Though she tried, she could see nothing. No shape, no form.

Nothing but black.

A smothering blanket of it.

She was fully awake when she heard her name again. Slowly she turned toward the window, and the sound. Cold eyes in a face she could not see stared back at her.

She swallowed hard and blindly felt for the keypad of the phone she had recently discarded. She needed help. But the eyes in the formless face said no. She peered again into the darkness and this time she glimpsed a nose, a line of jaw, a curve of brow.

"Oh my God," she said out loud.

It was Turner.

Hannah scrambled from the bed. Her brother hadn't been murdered or kidnapped or driven to a desert and left to die. Her brother was OK.

Her brother was here.

And a moment after her joy, she realized that something was terribly wrong. Turner shouldn't be at her cottage in the middle of the night.

She raced to the living room, pulled back the heavy oak front door and tugged her brother inside. He collapsed on a straight chair near the entrance.

"Shut it," he said. His voice was hoarse and tired. "And bolt it."

But Hannah was staring at her brother, a limp and

bleeding form folded carelessly on the stiff wooden chair beside her door.

"Do it," he said. "Now."

And blindly Hannah obeyed.

The door bolted, she turned back to her brother. Turner's face was battered and dirty and the skin under his left eye was quickly darkening. He tried to straighten up, or maybe to stand, but fell back against the chair with a soft groan. With one hand he clutched his left shoulder and between his fingers trickled a small stream of blood.

He coughed once and then doubled over.

Confusion and fear momentarily paralyzed Hannah. "I'll get help," she told him, but he shook his head and she stopped.

"I just need a place to rest."

Hannah watched as he tried to stand. He levered himself using the massive door handle for balance. But once upright he evidently found it too difficult to walk and collapsed again onto the stiff wooden chair.

"Let's get you to the couch," she said and tugged him to his feet. Putting his arm across her shoulder, she led him across her living room to the sofa. A moment later he was leaning back with his eyes closed.

Quiet filled the room, broken only by the occasional groan from her brother. Hannah was no good at triage. He looked awful, for sure, but she had seen him looking worse. He had been beaten up pretty badly when he was a junior in high school. That time the class giant had kicked him around the soccer field instead of a ball because he wouldn't hand over his car keys. Maybe all he needed was a little rest.

Turner's face was swelling rapidly and his left eye wore an angry bruise that spread toward his nose. "You need ice on that," she said and started toward the kitchen.

"Let it be," he said.

"I want to get the swelling down on your face," she told him.

His eyes fluttered shut. Then he tried to pull in a long breath but winced instead and started coughing.

Hannah could only stare.

"I need a drink," he told her.

"Are you cut?" she asked and nodded toward his shoulder.

"Not cut."

He was as cryptic as Jesher. "Then what?"

"How about that drink? I could really use something."

"Drink? I'm done with you, Turner Swift," she said. "You come to my house at two in the morning, half beaten to death, you won't let me help you and all you can say is you want a drink."

"Shot," he said.

"Well you're not getting one here. Not a shot of anything until you tell me what happened."

"I was shot."

Hannah dropped to a chair while the enormity of his words sank in. "Shot?" She looked over at her brother who had started to shake. Then she stood and walked into her bedroom.

"What are you doing?"

"I'm getting dressed. And then I'm getting you some help."

"No," Turner said.

"Turner, I can't help you. You need a doctor," she told him. But Turner was already shaking her off.

"Look," she said, "whatever kind of trouble you're in can't be as bad as bleeding to death or getting gangrene from a gunshot wound. You need medical attention, and I can't give it." As she watched, Turner's head bobbed toward his chest. A moment later he forced his head up, his eyes open.

"Then find someone who can," Turner replied. He leaned his head back against the sofa and his eyes rolled shut.

Hannah watched while her brother drifted away from her. "Turner," she said when she could find her voice. But his eyes were closed and the tremor in his hand refused to stop. She had to keep him from whatever fog was claiming his consciousness. "Turner," she said again and a moment later his pale eyes fluttered open.

"Get someone," he muttered. "Unless you want to dig around in my arm for the ammo yourself." He stopped speaking and licked at his swollen lips.

"I'll get you some water," Hannah told him.

"Forget the water. Get somebody to patch me up." He let his head fall back against the wall with a dull thud and his eyes closed again.

Just the same, Hannah went to the kitchen and drew some cool water into a glass. It gave her a chance to think. But time bought her nothing. She didn't know anyone who could remove a bullet and sew together the jagged pieces of flesh torn open from a gunshot. She knew art dealers and potters and sculptors. She walked back to the foyer and, kneeling beside her brother, offered him the water.

He drank deeply and when he was finished he turned his pale eyes on his sister. "Did you make a call?"

Hannah shook her head. "I'm taking you to Memorial," she told him. "It's the only thing to do."

"No," her brother said. "I told you, no hospitals. Doctors have to report gunshot wounds to the police. It's the law."

"Then what, Turner? What do you want me to do? I won't let my own brother bleed out in my living room while I watch." She took the empty glass from his hand. "And I don't know anyone who can put you back together again."

"What about Kenyon? You two looked cozy. And I'm betting he isn't as clean as you think. He'll know somebody who can do it. Call him."

Hannah didn't move. Jesher wouldn't know what to do any more than she did. He traded art, expensive art, maybe even dubiously obtained art, but he didn't know anyone who would dig a bullet out of someone's flesh and then keep quiet about it.

At least she didn't think he did.

The notion that her brother intuitively knew this much about the man who had taken her in her own kitchen tore at Hannah in ways she could not manage. She shook it off, refusing to give space to the unsettling idea.

"I said, get him," Turner said.

Her brother's voice was loud but it wasn't strong and Hannah sensed that he would soon be unconscious. "I'll call him," she said, finally, "but I'm not sure he'll help."

"He'll help all right. I saw the way he looked at you. He'll do it for you," Turner said and slipped lower on the couch. "He'll do it for you."

Hannah picked up the phone and dialed Jesher's private number.

He answered on the first ring.

"It's Hannah," she told him. "My bro – "

But Turner was shaking her off.

"Can you come over here? Now?" She looked helplessly at her brother. "I need you," she added a moment later.

The phone went dead in her hand.

"Is he coming?" Turner asked.

"I don't know," she told him.

Ten minutes later she heard the soft purr of an engine just outside her door. Hannah had cut away the sleeve on Turner's shirt to reveal a nasty wound in his upper arm. She had managed to slow the bleeding with some pressure, but the wound still oozed endlessly from a body that had lost its battle with consciousness.

There was a soft knock at the door and Turner stirred, struggling to open his eyes.

"It's Jesher," she said.

"Be sure."

But Hannah had no way to do that. Instead she went with her instinct and, unbolting the door, pulled it open.

Jesher stepped inside.

Even as she watched, he sized up the situation and the expression on his face slipped from sensual anticipation to blatant surprise. "Turner," he said softly and waited while the young man dragged himself back to consciousness. "Any other wounds?"

Turner blinked deeply, then screwed his face into something that passed for a smile. "Only my pride," he managed and before he had finished speaking, Jesher was tugging him to his feet.

"I've got to get you to better light," Jesher said. "See if you can stand."

Hannah raced to her brother's side and together they brought him to the kitchen. Jesher pulled a chair away from the table and pushed it up to the wall. Then the two of them lowered Turner onto it.

"Get towels," Jesher said, "and something to use for bandages." Then he started rummaging through the drawers by the sink.

But Hannah stood frozen while a surreal scene played out in her kitchen.

"Hannah!" Jesher said. "The towels."

A moment later she had gathered towels, packets of gauze and three ace bandages she had bought when she had sprained her ankle. On one finger dangled two unopened rolls of adhesive tape.

When she came back into the kitchen, Jesher was kneeling beside her brother, gently probing the wound with one finger, all the while speaking softly to him.

"You're lucky," he said finally. "There's no bullet. But we've got to get this cleaned and make sure the bleeding stops." He looked up at Hannah. "I need antiseptics. What do you have? Hydrogen peroxide, Betadine?"

"I've got alcohol and some Iodine."

"It's a start. Get that and anything else you can find."

Within minutes, Hannah was back, her hands full of any topical medication she could dig out of her medicine chest. She dumped them all on the kitchen table.

Jesher was still kneeling beside her brother and dabbing at the edges of the wound with a corner of a towel. He looked up and nodded his thanks.

"Why don't you go in the other room?" he suggested. "There's nothing you can do here."

But Hannah didn't budge.

Turner dragged open his eyes. His ashen skin looked damp, almost oily. "What he says, Hannah," he said in his toughest voice. "Just do it." Then his eyes fluttered shut.

Hannah looked helplessly from her semi-conscious

brother to Jesher. Finally she nodded.

"Put on some music," Jesher added. "Something upbeat."

Hannah was way past questioning Jesher. The adrenaline that had exploded within her body had long since retreated, leaving her trembling uncontrollably. Obediently she walked into the living room and found a rock station on her radio.

"Good," Jesher called from the kitchen when the music started. "But turn it up, I can barely hear it."

Hannah hit the volume knob. A peppy little number by some boy band fairly shook the room. She sank onto the sofa and allowed the snappy tune with its close harmony to wrap itself around her. Jesher was in control; everything would be all right. She closed her eyes and lay back against the sofa.

A moment later she went rigid.

A strangled sound that refused to be masked by the blaring music poured from the kitchen. She shot off the sofa. "Turner?"

"He's fine," came Jesher's calm voice. "Tell her you're fine."

"I'm fine," Turner said.

Hannah believed none of it. She walked to the kitchen door where she found Jesher bending over her brother, an open bottle of alcohol in his hand. Her brother's tightly clenched jaw was quivering. "Get out of here, Sis." He swallowed back a gag. "I mean it."

Hannah turned away. Twice more she heard the stifled noise that froze her blood, the last one followed by a string of oaths in Farsi, French and one other language she couldn't identify.

"We're fine. Almost done. Change the station, why don't you?" Jesher called. "Something quiet."

Hannah found the local jazz station and turned down the volume. Then she walked to the kitchen and stood at the door. The room was a mess. Blood had dripped onto the floor and the table and was already starting to coagulate. Her simple tan towels were soaked in it. And her brother looked ready to retch. Sweat sluiced down his chiseled cheekbones and gathered at his throat.

She started toward him.

Jesher looked up. "Leave, Hannah," he said softly. "Go back into the living room and sit down."

She didn't move.

"Now," he told her.

She heard her brother set free another string of oaths as she turned and walked out of the kitchen. A short time later Jesher joined her.

"He needs rest," Jesher said. "Your room OK?"

Hannah nodded. "Will he be all right?"

"I cleaned everything out and closed it with some butterflies and a bandage, but he needs professional help - ten or twelve stitches, I'd guess, and better trained eyes than mine, to be sure the wound is clean."

"He won't go."

"His call."

Hannah worried a look at Jesher.

"He may have some broken ribs, too. It looks like

he was kicked." Jesher took off his glasses and rubbed the bridge of his nose. Then he carefully replaced them, hooking the golden wires behind his ears.

"Did he say who did this to him?" Hannah asked.

Jesher shook his head. "Too dark. Anyway, he was hit from behind. Help me get him to bed," he added after a moment. "Right now he's dead weight."

How they got Turner into her tall brass bed Hannah wasn't quite sure, but before she had pulled up the thin cotton blankets, his eyes were closed. Hannah stood for a moment by the side of the bed and Jesher let her.

Her brother looked terrible. His black eye showed all the more prominently against skin now grayed from pain and loss of blood. And he seemed thin to her, and worn out. Turner had grown too intense for his own good and now it was eating him alive. She waited until his breathing steadied and when she was satisfied that he wouldn't die immediately she left the room.

Jesher had found a classical station on her sound system and turned down the volume. He was in her kitchen scrubbing her floor to rid it of her brother's blood. For a time Hannah stood in the doorway just watching him. His shoulders and back flexed with every movement, bunching into hard muscles and then smoothing.

"I don't know how to thank you," she said after a time.

Jesher finished what he was doing and when the

floor was clean, he gathered the towels, tossed them into a dark green garbage bag and set it by the door.

Hannah collapsed onto the sofa. She felt weak and light headed.

"Adrenaline does its job," Jesher said, kneeling beside her, "but it leaves the shakes when it finally goes. Are you cold?"

"A little," she said.

He reached for her afghan and snuggled it around her. Then he stepped back into the kitchen and returned a short time later with two steaming mugs of tea.

The night had turned Hannah fragile. Her skin seemed oddly transparent and her brow was furrowed with concern for her brother. Jesher didn't miss the tremble in her fingers as she reached for the mug of tea.

"It's hot," he told her.

"I know," she said. She took a sip anyway and then set the mug on her coffee table. "You saved my brother's life tonight. How can I ever thank you?"

"Any idea what happened?" Jesher asked.

"He wouldn't say but it could be anything. Trouble found him when he was overseas working for AmRaq Oil." She shrugged. "Who knows what has happened since he came home. He isn't real chatty, in case you haven't noticed."

"You think it's that, then? AmRaq?"

"What else could it be?"

When Jesher didn't answer right away, Hannah's

head came up slowly and met his eyes in a quiet stare. "You're not thinking he had something to do with the Blochet, are you?" Anger rose in her throat and threatened to choke off further conversation.

"I'm not accusing him of anything. I'm saying this: the man's been shot and he doesn't want the authorities involved. That usually adds up to trouble. Now he's under your roof. Being here is not safe for you any more." Jesher let the words sink in and felt Hannah tighten down in her woolen cocoon.

He wanted to lift her onto his lap, to brush aside her fears and tell her that everything would be all right. But she wouldn't want any such act from him. Under the best of circumstances she was not the kind of woman who craved sweet lies. And these circumstances were anything but good. And so, instead, he contented himself with watching the soft overhead light raise sparkles in her shiny hair, and with smelling the scent of her shampoo. He drew in a long breath and felt a shudder deep in his chest.

"It won't be a problem," she said. "Turner won't stay here. As soon as he can stand, he'll be gone."

"That changes nothing. He's contacted you. So, now you're involved with whatever it is, whether you want to be or not."

"Then you are, too."

"It looks that way."

CHAPTER TEN

Jesher set his cup on the coffee table and stood. Turner Swift had become a problem. The plan had been to keep him close by offering him a job in security. That way Jesher could order a background check, fingerprint him, hell, even tail him if he deemed it necessary. Now he questioned the wisdom of his decision. Turner was trouble. And if trouble had found Hannah's brother, it would soon enough find her as well.

On the couch Hannah stirred and opened her eyes.

"I didn't mean to wake you," he said.

"I wasn't asleep." She sat up straight. "I'm worried about Turner."

"I am, too."

"Do you think he knows who shot at him?"

Jesher raised an eyebrow. "I think he knows more than he's saying. That's for sure."

Sometime earlier when Hannah had dozed off, Jesher had peeled off his blood spattered T-shirt and tossed it into the bag with the towels. Now he was standing before her seemingly unaware that he was partially dressed. Or maybe he was just that comfortable in his own skin. Either way, the effect on Hannah was the same. She swallowed and forced her eyes just past his hard abdomen and the fine line of black hair that started at his navel and disappeared beneath the low belt line of his underwear.

"Where's your shirt?" she asked.

The question caught Jesher off guard. He glanced down at himself almost as if he was surprised to see his T-shirt was gone. "It's dirty," he told her because dirty sounded better than bloody.

Jesher felt in his pocket for his keys. "I need to clean up. Are you O.K. here?"

"I'm fine," she said. Then she moved and the afghan slid from her shoulders.

Jesher leaned forward to cover her up and was ambushed by the scent of citrus and rosemary. He felt himself stir and straightened up. "You'll be all right?" he asked again.

She nodded. "Go. Change."

* * *

Hannah jerked awake to the sound of Jesher swearing. Sleep had taken her moments after he had left. Now he stood at the doorway to her bedroom. He swore again, something base and crude. She'd just bet Simona had never heard him talk like that.

Hannah sat up. "He's gone, isn't he?"

Jesher dragged his hand through his hair. Then he nodded. "My mistake. I didn't figure he'd bolt in the middle of the night." He rubbed his eyes. "I shouldn't have left."

Hanna was fully awake now. She stared into the grey morning beyond her windows and let the ramifications of her brother's departure sink in. Turner needed medical attention. He had been shot and beaten. But of greater concern to her was the fact that her brother was in trouble. The kind of trouble where people carried guns and used them. And those people were still out there.

"You can't stay here. This place," Jesher was saying, "is too unprotected."

Hannah shook her head. "It's private property. It's gated, for heaven's sake. I'd call that protected."

"That didn't stop your brother from getting in. Twice. I'm moving you to the main house."

"No. No. No," she said and stood, letting the afghan fall to the floor. "You're not moving me anywhere."

Jesher leveled a hard look right at her. "The main house, or my place. You choose. And do it now or I'll decide for you."

"What about Turner?"

"What about him? He's on his own."

Hannah felt sick. "You can't mean that. He's my brother and he's hurt."

"He's also the one who left. We can't do anything more for him."

"Shouldn't we call the police?"

"And tell them what? That your adult brother left in the middle of the night?" He shook his head again. "Let it alone, Hannah. There's nothing you can do." He started toward the kitchen. "I'll make some coffee. You start packing."

Hannah rubbed her eyes. "You're not serious."

Jesher turned slowly to face her. "Your brother

was beaten up and shot. He came to your house. What do you think?" He took in her face and read all the confusion and concern he saw there. He had frightened her and he hadn't meant to. He folded her in his arms and brushed the hair from her eyes. Then he dropped his voice until it was just a whisper. "Pack, Hannah."

By the time the coffee was ready, Hannah had put a nightgown, a few changes of underwear and some cosmetics into a duffle bag. She brought it into the living room and set it by the door next to the garbage bag of towels, a grim reminder of the night before.

Jesher came out of the kitchen with two steaming mugs of coffee. He urged one on Hannah, and then slouched onto the couch, his long legs pressing against the edge of the coffee table. "Is that all you're taking?" He nodded in the direction of her bag.

"It's a start. I'll come back for more if I need to."

"You're not coming back."

Hannah set down her mug and turned to the man beside her. "Good grief, Jesher. You're turning this whole affair into a spy thriller. Nobody is after me. No attack has been made on my life. There is no risk here. My brother is not a criminal and I'm not harboring him." She paused for a breath. "I've only agreed to go to the main house to humor you, you know."

Jesher's expression remained grim. "Get changed. I'm going to nose around outside." He stood and walked out of the cottage.

Simona was waiting at the front door of the main

house when they arrived half an hour later. While Jesher's clothes were clean, he had an uncharacteristically rumpled look. He wore a white dress shirt, half buttoned, and faded jeans, torn at one knee. He needed a shower and a shave. But if Simona noticed the dark stubble on his face and wrinkles in his clothes, she chose not to mention them.

"I'm putting you in the north wing," was all she said. Then she turned and led them both up the grand staircase, her cinnamon colored caftan floating behind her. She never asked why Hannah would be staying with her, or for how long. Knowing more wasn't necessary. Guests were always welcome at her home, including Alistair who still occupied a suite in the south wing. And she had raised her children to feel the same way.

Hannah's room was above the library, facing the circular driveway. It was a spacious room all done up in shades of pale blue. While the decor was tasteful, the room held a certain frilliness that bore no likeness to Hannah. There were ruffles. Lots and lots of ruffles. And a hand crocheted bed spread so finely done it looked like lace. Throw pillows laden with bows were mounded on bed, window seat and rocker. The effect was cloying.

Hannah took her bag from Jesher. "Thanks," she said. She waggled the small duffle at him. "This is all I'll need. Your mother won't stand for me staying here very long. She likes her independence and she likes her privacy. I'll be in her way inside of a day." She dropped the bag next to the rocker and walked to the full-length windows that flanked a huge mahogany bureau. "It's pretty here," she said, almost to herself. "I've never been above the first floor." Then she rubbed at the tight muscles in her neck, trying to free a knot.

Jesher was over-reacting. No one was after her. Turner had likely gotten himself embroiled in some bar fight over a game of pool and had found himself at the wrong end of a gun. She knew her brother. He was forever getting in the middle of situations before he realized there wasn't any way out. He had always been scrappy. He had always found trouble. And he had never figured out when or how to get out of its way. She rubbed again at her neck.

Jesher's hand closed over hers and Hannah swallowed hard.

"You must have slept on it wrong," he told her, his voice just above a whisper.

"I didn't sleep," she told him. "I dozed."

"Dozed," he repeated. Then he pressed the tips of his fingers into the back of her neck and felt Hannah relax into his touch. "This was Lily's room when she came to live with us," he told her and lowered his fingers to the base of her neck. "But the ruffles were Mother's idea."

Jesher's had ceased massaging the knot in Hannah's neck, but his hand still rested on her shoulders. And now his fingers traced soft circles just above her collarbone. "Better?" he asked.

Hannah nodded.

"I know you don't want to be here, Hannah, but this isn't forever. Just until things get sorted out."

Where had she heard that before? "How long?" she asked.

"Not long," he told her. Then he slowly drew her to him and wrapped her in his arms.

There was something earthy about Hannah, something that he sensed was just beyond her understanding. Or her control. She responded to him sensually, completely. He drifted his fingers across the soft flesh of her throat and felt her shiver in response.

She turned in his arms until she could see his face. "This won't," she told him, "work. We made a mistake."

Jesher pressed his forefinger to her lips and when he had silenced her, he allowed his fingers to fall to the soft curve of her neck. He touched the smooth skin he found there and felt, rather than heard Hannah sigh.

"The only mistake," he said against her skin, "was that I went too fast." His fingers worked the tiny mother-of-pearl buttons of her blouse. "I want you slowly. I want to kiss you where you have never been kissed before. I want to kiss you in ways you can't even imagine. I want to be inside you and feel you around me. I want to hear you tell me you're ready to explode and then I want to feel you do just that."

Hannah shook her head and stepped away from him. She needed distance from a man who would say such things to her. "I won't do it again," she told him.

"I won't sleep with you."

"We don't have to sleep," he offered.

"Don't make light of the situation, Jesher, I'm serious. It was just sex between us and I won't do it. Not again. Not with you. Not ever."

"Then we won't call it sex."

"Give it any moniker you want," she said. Exasperation edged her voice. "It can't happen between us again."

"And why is that?"

"Because that's all there is. Just sex."

"So you say."

"And you to say there's more? You're sticking to me like a cheap suit in the rain only because you think I'm involved in the theft of the Blochet. If it weren't for the missing statue, this . . ." she paused, making a weak gesture between their bodies while she hunted down the right word.

"Sex?" he offered.

Hannah nodded and turned away from the man who made her want. "If it weren't for the theft, this sex between us never would have happened. It was just something to do while you keep me here."

"Is that what you really think?"

"Tell me otherwise. You've refused to write my letter of reference. You as much as told me you think I know more than I'm telling." She swung around to face him. "Go ahead. Deny it."

Silence deadened the room.

Hannah felt sick. "Please leave," she told him. "I

can't give you what you want. I won't."

"And what is it I want?"

"A fling," she shot back. "An amusement. Something to pass the time until this mess with the Blochet is sorted out."

"You're no fling."

"Of course I am."

"And how is it you know what I want?"

"Well, it isn't any secret. I practically live with your family. I even come to family gatherings. Lily is your biggest advocate, you know. She was quite clear."

"Was she?"

"And I see her point. You haven't exactly had positive role models for monogamous relationships."

Beside her Jesher took off his glasses and rubbed his eyes. "I could do without the psychoanalysis," he said slowly. "Nobody knows my mind. Not Lily and not you. You don't know how I feel about my father. You can't even figure out how I feel about you. We're good together, Hannah Swift. I'm guessing that's hard for you to admit, because when you're with me you're a different person. Still, it's out there and you need to take a long, hard look at it." He paused on his way to the door and then without turning around, he added, "Let me know when you've figured it all out." Behind him the door slammed shut.

* * *

The ride in Jesher's Land Rover was no more

comfortable on this day than it had been a month before. He had come by the main house just before noon and told Simona he was borrowing Hannah. Half an hour later the two of them were riding along an unpaved bit of road not far from Lake Ontario. Wind whipped through the interior of the truck and chilled her, despite the warm spring sun that had finally returned.

"I feel kidnapped," she told Jesher.

"Don't. It's lunch, not a felony," he replied. He let his eyes leave the road and drift over the small woman next to him. He had no way to know how she would respond to him today.

"Where are we going?"

"To the beach. Lots of people around. Couldn't be safer."

"Why am I not comforted?"

Jesher shrugged and hit the gas. The Land Rover skidded momentarily before gripping the surface of the road.

"Besides," she added a moment later, "there won't be any people at the beach today. It's barely May."

"There will be enough."

"For what?"

But Jesher evidently decided against responding to her question.

Hannah could only stare. "So we're right back in the spy thriller again, aren't we? Public place, no bugs. Am I right?"

Jesher looked over at her briefly. Then he put his

eyes back on the road and sped toward the public beach.

The beach at Lake Ontario was always an unexpected pleasure for Hannah. In her youth the area had become first merely run-down, and then eventually home to some unsavory characters. But more recently the original public buildings, dating back to the Victorian era, had been carefully restored. Bath houses, lodges and shelters dotted the shoreline. And at the north end of the beach, the public breakwater and pier jutted well into the waters of lake.

Jesher pulled his truck into a spot not far from the century-old Merry-Go-Round and killed the engine. "First, lunch. I'm starved." He loosened his tie, took off his suit jacket and folded it over his arm. Though his suit was a conservative gabardine, the lining, when the sunlight hit it, fairly dazzled. The brilliant silk linings, this one stripes of mauve, lavender and green, were the signature of a local tailor who had made his mark dressing the gargantuan bodies of football players and such.

Jesher took her lightly by the elbow and steered her toward a small beachside stand. He ordered two hotdogs, and handed one to Hannah.

"Let's walk," he said and took a bite, nodding in the direction of the pier. Spring had been slow to arrive and, although the sun was bright, a cool Canadian wind whipped the lake into frothy peaks. Gulls glided overhead, shrieking at the few people who had stolen time from lunch to enjoy the view.

Half way to the end of the pier, the walkway widened enough to offer benches. Jesher found an empty one and sat.

"How's lunch?" he asked when Hannah was seated next to him. "You have to have hot dogs at the beach."

Hannah nodded.

"I got an interesting call this morning."

The comment sounded conversational. Except Hannah knew it wasn't. Jesher didn't idle over polite social patter.

"Turner?" she asked. "Did he contact you? Is he all right?"

"I haven't heard from Turner." He stopped speaking and scanned the immediate area. Then he lowered his voice. "This was about the Blochet."

Jesher had said he would know if the statue became available. Evidently he was right.

"The call was an offer to sell." He let the words sink in before going on. "Not a source I knew, though that isn't always a deal breaker." He finished off his lunch and tossed the thin paper plate and napkin into a trash container at his left.

Hannah took a long breath. This was where she should tell him about Turner's voice mail, the one where he hinted that there might be some trouble with the Blochet. But she said nothing.

"I mentioned that I might have a buyer," Jesher was saying. "Of course I would need to see the item. The seller knows that."

Hannah set the remainder of her hot dog on the bench beside her. "Which one, exactly, is for sale?"

"It'll be interesting to find out, don't you think?"

Hannah shook her head. This wasn't interesting. This was scary stuff. This was big time art theft. The kind that got people killed and dumped into land fills, or covered with cement. "Why would anyone call and tell you it's on the market? The Blochet is already yours."

"True, but I can't sell it. Grandfather Woolley saw to that."

Hannah remembered. Possession of *L'homme Ordinaire* was to follow Woolley bloodlines to the fourth generation. That meant Jesher. That also meant he couldn't sell it even if he wanted to. Unless it was stolen and showed up on the black market.

"The people I do business with know the story, too, which is why this is so interesting." Jesher reached into the breast pocket of his jacket and pulled out several papers that had been lightly folded lengthwise. "These arrived this morning by messenger."

A few people had joined them on the pier – an older couple and two women with a small tan dog on a leash. He handed the papers to Hannah. "Have a look," he said.

Hannah took the papers and opened them up. There were four pages of images, pictures of *L'homme Ordinaire* taken at various angles. But the shots were anything but clear. It appeared that they had been taken from a distance, or through glass. She sifted through the photos, returning several times to the third one. "It's hard to . . ."

With a single shake of his head, Jesher motioned her quiet. "I agree." He held out his hand for the photos and, folding them just as they had been, slipped them back into his coat pocket.

The photos were of a Blochet, but real or copy was anyone's guess. Hannah hoped that Jesher was bringing her into his circle to elicit her help. But she just wasn't sure.

"You finished?" He picked up her half-eaten hot dog and tossed it, along with the napkins into the trash. "Let's get some coffee. You look cold."

They found a coffee shop not far from the pier and a small table right in the middle of the crowd. Jesher motioned for her to sit.

Moment later he set a steaming latte in front of her. "Can we talk about this?" she asked.

He shrugged. "I don't know anything more. I can't be certain what's for sale. I don't know who has it, or how it was obtained."

"So you could be buying the real one?"

"Right."

To Hannah he seemed calm, maybe even confident about dealing with criminals. She found the notion unnerving.

"I'm going to contact the seller," he went on, "and find out when the item will be available. That should give us some answers."

"In the meantime?"

"The exhibit ends this Friday. Dismantling should start right after closing. I'm sending a security team to oversee packing and to escort the pieces back to the States."

And in the meantime, she knew she wouldn't be leaving Pinehurst.

The ride back to the family estate was managed in relative silence while Hannah mulled over several possible outcomes to the events that were unfolding. She could only guess what occupied Jesher's thoughts.

Half an hour later they pulled into the circular drive at the main house. Jesher let the engine idle while Hannah gathered up her belongings. The quiet ride home, she had to admit, had finally gotten to her. Twice she had glanced at Jesher, but his eyes were masked behind sunglasses, his expression hidden from her. It was good to be back where she could escape to her own thoughts.

Hannah offered a courteous thanks for lunch and lifted the door latch. Too late she remembered that it required more muscle than she had to open it. For a moment she stilled in her seat, refusing to ask for help and unable to leave without it.

"It sticks," Jesher reminded her and reached across her, brushing lightly against her with his forearm. He gave the door a whack with the heel of his hand. But he didn't seem in a hurry to move, stretched across Hannah as he was.

Hannah pulled in a slow breath and caught his scent, freshly starched shirt and warm wool with something else she couldn't name.

"This isn't settled between us, Hannah Swift," he said against her ear, "just because you say it is." His breath ruffled the curls that had strayed from her French braid and sent a shiver tracing down her spine. He let his tongue drift against her neck, breathing in the citrus and lavender that hid there. Then he straightened away from her. "Not settled at all."

Again Hannah shivered.

"Good. You're back," Simona said as she stepped into the bright afternoon sunlight.

Jesher smoothly pulled away from Hannah and straightened into his seat.

"I told him to wait," Simona was saying. She hooked her arm through Hannah's just as she slid from the truck, and led her toward the house. A moment later Simona stopped and turned back to her son. "Jesher? A moment please, if you can spare the time."

Jesher turned off the engine and stepped out of the truck. "Problem, Mother?"

"I hope not. Just the bank. Could you be a dear and talk to Larry Woodrow again?" Then she put her arm through her son's and led her son and his lover into the foyer of Pinehurst.

It was dark inside the massive house and it smelled of lemon oil. Hannah heard a familiar voice and, looking about, found Turner pacing in the formal living room. His left arm was bound up in a black orthopedic sling and in his right hand he held his phone. He was nodding endlessly as if the phone could recognize the gesture. He looked tight and impatient.

"I know," he said finally. "I'm on it." He turned, and seeing Hannah and Jesher, disconnected and dumped the phone into his pocket. A few strides carried him to the foyer. He held out his right hand. "Jesher," he said, "good to see you."

"You look well," Jesher said, not missing a beat.

But to Hannah it seemed that trouble still wore at her brother's face, forming tiny lines at his eyes and making his cheeks hollow and dark.

"I got some stitches." Turner said, lifting his left arm slightly, "and it's healing, so that's good. Thanks for your help."

Thanks? That was it? Hannah wanted to shake her brother. She wanted to yell at him the same way her mother had when he was a boy. Jesher had cleaned him up, bound him up, and probably saved his life. Being a bit more effusive wouldn't kill him, not one bit.

And more, Hannah wanted to know what had possessed Turner to leave her cottage in the middle of the night when he had been so weak. She wanted to know where he had gone and how he had gotten there. And most of all she wanted to know who had shot him. Because she sensed Turner knew.

"You weren't at your office so I came here looking for you," Turner was saying. "Your mother was nice enough to invite me in."

"We're about to have tea in the garden." Simona

walked up to Turner and patted his hand. "Hannah? Jesher? Will you be joining us?"

"Mother, I have business with Turner. Something that needs attention now. Could you give us a few minutes?" And without waiting for a reply, he ushered Hannah and Turner into the library.

If Hannah had thought recent events to have knocked some of the cockiness from her brother she was wrong. His walk was a challenge to any nearby male who thought to best him. His facial expression was an outright dare. Hannah sank into one of the leather club chairs, hoping she wasn't about to witness a cockfight. Her brother knew how to draw lines in the dirt and Jesher wasn't afraid to cross them.

Jesher pulled shut the mahogany pocket doors and sat as well.

"I'm glad to see you're doing better, Turner," Jesher said. "And I'm glad you had someone look at your shoulder. How does it feel?"

The chatty nature of Jesher's conversation came as a surprise to Hannah. She was certain she had never heard him utter socially polite inquiries, though she knew he had been raised to do so.

"I'll live," Turner said. "Another week, then the stitches come out and I get rid of the sling."

"Good," Jesher said. "Feeling up to work?"

There it was. It felt almost soothing to Hannah to know that Jesher hadn't slipped out of character.

"That's why I came looking for you. To tell you that I'm ready to do whatever you want."

"What I want is for you to oversee my security. That was the plan when I hired you. Nothing has changed." Jesher paused and pulled his phone from his pocket. A moment later he returned it. "This Friday Dewald will be dismantling the exhibit at the Vic. I'm sending you in a car."

"You got it."

Hannah shifted in her chair, making the old brown leather crackle. Something about her brother's demeanor was unsettling.

"I want you to check each piece against a list I will give you," Jesher was saying. "Dewald's people will do the packing but you are there to observe. If you have any questions, if you think anything isn't right, you call me right away."

"Understood."

Jesher continued as if Turner hadn't spoken. "Once everything is loaded, you are to accompany the pieces back to Pinehurst. If the items are opened at customs, I want the names and badge numbers of the officers."

Turner nodded.

"And I want you to check in with me every hour."

For a moment Turner's face held no expression at all. Then slowly it worked itself into a scowl. "And what if I forget?"

"You won't.

Turner stood, but his expression remained the same. "Is Hannah coming with?"

"No. Hannah will be here at Pinehurst with me."

There was a heartbeat of silence, broken only by

the steady ticking of the mantel clock.

Finally Turner spoke. "Divide and conquer. Is that the plan, then?"

For a moment Hannah thought she saw Jesher's face darken down. But then, like summer clouds, it cleared.

CHAPTER ELEVEN

Hannah pushed her chair back from the desk and walked to the front window. In the circular drive, Jesher's Jaguar waited obediently. Jesher was making good on his word to wait for Turner to bring *L'homme Ordinaire* home.

Hannah found Jesher in the study. He was seated on a leather sofa, his bare feet propped against a low, brass chest that served as a coffee table. An open laptop sat next to his feet and beside that, his phone. As she watched from the door, he typed something into his laptop, then closed it and leaned back against the sofa.

Hannah knocked gingerly on the partially open door, and when Jesher didn't look up, she knocked again. The second time he turned toward the noise, his brow crinkled at the distraction. An instant later his expression softened and he motioned her into the room.

"I see you haven't escaped," he noted and tossed a pencil onto the glass-topped surface of the brass chest.

"Not yet," she returned, "but I'm working on it."

He took off his glasses and, leaning forward, dropped them on top of his work. "I'm sure you are," he returned and allowed a minimal smile. "Come in," he said, "and sit." He patted the empty space next to him.

"There's something I need to tell you," she said and seated herself across from him instead. It was a beginning, however lame. Jesher needed to know.

"A confession?"

"Of sorts, I guess," she returned. Then she sucked in a long breath and plunged ahead. "I didn't say anything earlier because," she paused and searched for the right words, "well, you'll understand why when I tell you." She looked at Jesher, hoping for some kind of reassurance from him that all would be well.

She got none.

But if he wasn't talking, he was speaking with his eyes. Those endlessly green eyes roved about her, taking her in with unrepentant pleasure. He paused at her lips, dampening his own with the tip of his tongue as if ready to taste her. Then he lowered his gaze to her throat and her small rounded breasts that rose and fell rapidly with her growing unease. He could take her apart in a heartbeat with those deep pools of green. She wondered if he knew. At last, as if satisfied that the woman before him truly was the Hannah Swift he knew and not some imposter, he returned his gaze to her eyes.

"What is it that I will understand?" he asked. His voice was barely above a whisper.

"I got a voicemail from Turner."

Jesher leaned forward. "He is supposed to contact me, not you. He knows that."

"Not today, a few days ago." She took her phone from her pocket. "Before he was shot." She swiped the mail icon and handed her phone to Jesher. A moment later, the message played.

"You and me, we could be in some really deep shit. I met a guy who knows some stuff, stuff about those pieces we took to Toronto. If this dude's got the song right, . . . Christ, Hannah, why can't you just be there when I need you?"

Hannah glanced at Jesher's face but it held no expression at all. "I never did find out what he meant. I tried to call him back, but he had turned off his phone and . . ." She shrugged. "The next time I heard from him, he was banging on my door in the middle of the night, bleeding."

Jesher shrugged. "We'll find out soon enough, I guess."

It was not the response she had expected.

Then he stood, and with that simple movement closed down any further tries at conversation. Hannah wondered if she had interrupted him at some crucial point in his business, though it hadn't appeared he was doing vital work. Perhaps he simply didn't want to talk. She gathered herself and stood as well, the folds of her soft lime skirt billowing to her knees as she did so.

Jesher felt a twinge of desire and fought it back. She couldn't know what she did to him or she would never smile at him that way, never bend so near to him the way she just had. He squeezed shut his eyes. He needed a run. A long one. Because he needed to rid himself of the tension this woman imposed, however unwittingly. He would run until he found the peace he needed. And he would do it just as soon as she was no longer in his presence. But then she passed in front of him and he caught her scent, all lime and, what was it this time? Coconut? He cleared his throat and moved toward the door.

Hannah paused and turned back to him. Her eyes were soft on his and he wondered if she knew how she made him feel. Probably not, he concluded, or she would never have come into the room, never have slipped past him so close that she had freshened the very air he breathed.

Jesher reached out for her slowly, halting her with his touch, and waited for any sign of resistance. He found none. Her flesh was soft and warm. He pushed aside his urge to drag her body against his and hold her so tightly he could feel her heartbeat through that flimsy blouse she wore. He had told her the next move was hers. He was good for his word.

Jesher let out a long, slow breath and released her arm.

"You're right, you know," Hannah said.

Jesher didn't respond.

"I am a different person with you."

She hadn't moved any closer to him, but neither had she retreated. Again Jesher reached out and this time rested his hand lightly on her shoulder.

"I'm not sure I want to be, but there it is, and I don't think there's anything I can do about it." The admission was oddly freeing, and with the saying of what she knew to be true, she moved closer to the man she wanted to hold her. She would sort through it later and maybe come to terms with it. But even if she never understood it, she knew one thing. She had to let her time with Jesher follow a natural course, or she would regret it the rest of her life.

She closed the space between them and sighed into his arms.

Jesher lowered his head and pressed his lips quietly against hers. At his barest touch she parted her mouth seeking and finding his tongue. She tasted sweet and warm. Jesher closed his eyes and pulled her against him close enough that finally he could feel the life force beating inside her.

"Hannah," he breathed all the while nibbling her unadorned ear. With Hannah he never knew if she was innately seductive or if she was purposely arousing him. Either way the result was the same. And, as if on cue, she moved against him. Immediately Jesher felt himself thicken. A moment later he was pushing uncomfortably against the confines of his jeans. He gritted his teeth and took a mental retreat. A moment more and he would be groping blindly for her, mindless of where they were. And that wasn't what he wanted for either of them.

This time he wanted her to be sure.

Jesher sucked in a long, shuddering breath, clearing the haze that was fast enveloping his brain. "Not here," he said.

Then he took her hand and brought her to her borrowed room on the second floor. "Better," he said and closed the door behind them. "More private."

Hannah came to him, her eyes wearing a hungry

look he longed to sate. And he would if he could keep his sanity long enough. But then her fingers grazed over the jutting stiffness of his erection. He groaned. Hannah fumbled at his fly, seeking a zipper and finding instead maddening metal buttons. He reached down and gently took her hand away.

"Not yet," he told her. "This time I want you slowly." His fingers worked quietly at the buttons of her blouse and then her skirt, ridding her of trappings useless for the world of love. When she wore nothing more than her lime green panties he took her to the bed and there he lay her down.

A moment later Jesher stood naked before her, lean and dark. He had had women of all kinds, from all kinds of places and he had made love in as many ways as he figured there were, and he had always remained the master of both the situation and himself. But Hannah stripped him of the control and that would never do. Jesher hovered above her momentarily, gathering in his resolve, because this time he wanted to show her the pleasure to be had from a slow cadence.

When he had reclaimed his control, he eased himself onto her. "Since the night of the gala," he said against her lips, "maybe before that, I have wanted you in every way that a man wants a woman." He planted kisses on her face and throat.

Slowly he eased his way down her slender form, leaving a trail of dark kisses behind. She was perfection, this tiny lady who now lay beneath him.

She was also, his saner self reminded him, a potential complication. She flickered with desire, imperfectly masked by personal goals and a life-map, and maybe much more than that. She was the poster child for all things practical, at least that was the message she offered. But, for the moment she was his. He would pleasure her now and deal with the less savory implications of Hannah Swift's presence in his life later. Much later.

"You're beautiful," he told her. And she was. The first time he had been in a crazed adolescent rush. He hadn't seen her, not really. Not like this. Hannah looked serene. Her pale eyes were hidden from him now, but her lips bore the look of succulent anticipation. Small, perfectly rounded breasts rose and fell with each breath she took and though he had barely touched her, the dark flesh of her nipples stood begging to be tasted. Jesher obliged. He placed his lips over her other breast tugging at her gently with his teeth.

Beneath him she squirmed and in so doing brushed herself against his throbbing erection. Jesher clenched his jaw and waited endless moments for the sensation that threatened to drive him over the edge to pass. He wanted to pleasure her, knowing that it would pleasure them both and that meant putting aside his own need.

With one hand he urged her legs apart and then opened her with his thumb. He had thought she would resist him; instead she moved against his hand, urging him to touch her again. She was wet already, and plump with desire. He slipped a finger inside her swollen channel and heard her breath quicken. He withdrew it and then slipped it in again, this time drawing out her dampness. She was slick and hot. She was ready for him. Jesher drove down the primitive urge to push himself into her and instead lowered his head and let his tongue sample the hot flesh he had exposed.

Hannah gasped and pulled away from him. Reluctantly he raised his lips.

"Don't think, just feel. Let it go, Hannah, and trust me."

She didn't answer, only sighed.

Jesher waited until he felt her relax before he once again lowered his head. This time he found the center of her desire. The soft convulsions began almost at once. She reached for him pressing his head into her, urging him to taste her again and again until he felt her at last slacken beneath him.

Only then did he rise above her and in a single stroke he pushed himself inside her. She was tight and hot and though she seemed without inhibition, he doubted she had been with many men. He withdrew partially before driving himself steadily back into her. This time he felt her tighten around him. The flesh of her channel pulled him in ever deeper as she clenched and pulsed about his swollen manhood. His world darkened, threatened to spin away from him as he wavered for a moment on the edge of endless pleasure.

He ground his teeth wanting desperately to hold back the moment. But it was already too late. He felt his world explode and with one final thrust he spilled himself into her.

* * *

Hannah stared out the kitchen window into the gathering darkness while Jesher busied himself stirring a pot of chicken soup. Her mood was grim. Jesher Kenyon was no one she should want. But she did. His curt exterior bore little resemblance to the man she had come to know. He was warm and caring, though he rarely showed it. And she had fallen in love with him despite her best efforts.

Hannah had known what she wanted for her life and had gone after it. Turner's insatiable need for ready cash had temporarily derailed her, but it hadn't dampened her drive. Until now. Now everything was different. Because now there was Jesher Kenyon.

She gave her head a little shake. She worried that she knew what Jesher was doing. She worried that he was keeping her close until the theft was solved. If it was ever solved. But most of all she worried that the rest of what was happening between them was just an amusement for him.

Across the room Jesher set down the wooden spoon and answered his phone. A moment later he set his phone back on the kitchen table. It pulsed momentarily before slipping into wait mode. "Turner is back in the States."

Hannah watched as he placed a steaming bowl of soup in front of her. She let out an audible sigh. "Finally. I was beginning to worry."

"Me, too," Jesher said.

Turner had called once before to let Jesher know the artifacts were packed, sealed and ready for transport. Then he had called again when he and his men were on the QE II, the main highway leading west to the border. Now he had passed through customs and soon the mystery surrounding the Blochet would be sorted out.

At least Hannah hoped it would.

Behind them the kitchen door swung open. "Really, Jesher. You were raised better." Simona surveyed her son and her personal assistant. "The family doesn't eat at the kitchen table."

Jesher stood and pulled out a chair for his mother. "Why don't you join us? We were just having some supper."

Simona hesitated at the door, as if she were about to enter a forbidden zone. Then evidently brushing protocol aside, she walked into the immense kitchen intended for a staff of four.

The kitchen almost ran the width of the house. Cabinets covered all of the walls and below them were stainless steel countertops. At one end was a pantry and at the other two commercial gas ranges. In the center of the oblong room was a scrubbed-top table, and around it several mismatched chairs. On most days, this was where the staff took their meals. But not tonight. Tonight the kitchen was empty.

"We found some soup. Would you like a bowl?"

Simona nodded and took a place next to her son.

"I let Jonathan and the others go early tonight," Jesher said. He set a bowl of hot chicken noodle soup in front of his mother and handed her a spoon and napkin.

"The soup is very good," Hannah said.

Simona took a sip and smiled at the couple seated opposite her. "I'll be happy to have *L'homme* back home again." She took another spoonful of soup and turned toward Jesher. "I should never have let the Blochet go, you know. I've thought and thought about it. Grandfather Woolley wouldn't be pleased."

"Mother, you did the right thing."

"Think how many people got to see him," Hannah said. "Otherwise they would never have had the chance. I'm glad you lent him to the Vic."

"I suppose you're right, dear," Simona said, "but I worried the whole time he was gone."

"Worried about what?" Hannah said.

"That something would happen to him. The Blochet was entrusted to my care and he has never been away from me."

Hannah was worried as well, but not about the Blochet's absence. She was worried about its return. She had no way of knowing how Simona would respond if the sculpture that her brother brought back wasn't the real *L'homme Ordinaire*. And if she had learned anything from the events at the Royal Victoria Museum's Gala, Jesher had no Plan B.

Simona ate in uncustomary silence, glancing at Jesher and Hannah between spoonsful of her soup. When she had finished eating, she set down her spoon and looked directly at her son.

"I'm going to my room, dear," she said.

Jesher couldn't mask his surprise. "Not waiting for *L'homme*?"

Simona shook her head. "I've got a lot of things to do. Arrangements to make." She stood. "You put him in the vault, in the back where I keep the study I made." She walked to her son and kissed him lightly on both cheeks. Then she turned to Hannah. "You see he does what I ask." She gave her a wink and left the kitchen.

Jesher gathered up the dishes and placed them in the sink. "Well, that simplifies things," he said. He squirted some dish detergent into the sink and waited for the stainless steel basin to fill with hot water. "Now I don't have to ask you to distract her."

Hannah's head shot up. "Like before at the Vic?"

Jesher smiled and started washing the bowls and spoons.

Less than half an hour later, a car pulled into the circular driveway.

Turner was back.

Jesher stood. "Wait in the study," he told her.

Hannah frowned.

But before she could say anything he added,

"Please." He waited while she left the kitchen and went into the study. Then he walked to the front of the house, pulled back the immense front door, and stepped into the darkness.

From the entrance to the study, Hannah could see the front door, but it was the silence that caught her attention. Endless quiet when there should have been the voices. And noise.

Movement.

Something.

Finally there was Jesher's voice. "Put the crates in the foyer. I'll take them from there."

She heard footfalls and then the front door closed.

In the following silence, Hannah waited. Minutes passed and the quiet began to close in on her. Jesher should be tearing at the crates. But he wasn't. Save for the distant electrical hum of some appliance, the whole house was still. Something wasn't right.

Hannah stepped from the study to the side hall and peered into the enormous foyer. Six wooden crates, all the same size, stood on the foyer floor, just inside the entryway. In the bank of leaded glass windows at the front of the house, she could see the outline of the town car that had brought Turner. Moments later headlights flashed across the lawn and the car pulled away.

And then Jesher was walking toward the study. His features looked dark.

Hannah met him half way there. "We need to unpack."

"I asked you to stay in the study."

"You're joking, right?" she returned.

Jesher stopped moving and turned to her. If his look was intended to intimidate, it sorely missed the mark. His pale eyes swept across her face, drinking in each feature, sip by sip before settling on her mouth. Something gentle smoothed out the serious expression his face. And then the gentleness was gone.

"Something happened," she told him. "What? Did something happen to Turner?" She scoured Jesher's face for answers.

"Turner is fine."

"Then what?"

"It's Edgar Dewald. Turner is concerned about him."

Hannah took a moment to process what Jesher had said. Hannah loved her brother but right now his life didn't hold many places for concern for others. Especially for someone he barely knew. "Concerned?" she said finally. "Why?"

"Turner said he didn't look well."

Hannah gave Jesher a frown.

"Beaten, actually." He squeezed shut his eyes as if he were warding off an oncoming headache. "Turner's words, not mine."

"You mean worn out?"

"No. With fists. Or a bat."

Hannah sank onto one of the chairs.

"He had a black eye and his lip was split."

"He's an old man. Maybe he fell."

"Maybe," Jesher said, "but Turner didn't seem to think so."

"Did he ask Dewald what had happened?"

He had asked, it turned out, but Dewald was not forthcoming. And even though Dewald had insisted the bruises and such were not recent, Hannah's brother had called for medical attention and stayed until it arrived.

And there stood the elephant in the room. Another beating delivered to someone associated with the Blochet. Jesher evidently didn't want to talk about it, so he busied himself momentarily by checking his messages. But Hannah had to know. "He was beaten like Turner was. What do you think is going on?"

Jesher shook his head. Then he pulled a box cutter from his front pocket and started toward the crates.

Attached to the top of each crate was a packing list sealed inside a clear plastic sleeve. Jesher slit open the sleeve on the end crate and pulled out the list.

Having found what he was after on the first attempt, Jesher slit the strapping tape that held the crate top in place. Then he plunged his hands into the froth of pale pink Styrofoam peanuts and felt around.

Beside him, Hannah waited. She watched carefully for any expression on Jesher's face. There was none. Slowly he raised the limestone head from its temporary home, bits of packing still clinging to it. Hannah thought how much this scene replicated the one she had witnessed at the Vic when Dr. Dewald had lifted the head so gingerly from its packing. She remembered with a shudder the bewilderment, and then the fear that had clawed at her when she realized it was a copy.

Jesher carried the head into the study and set it on the coffee table where he could examine it. Hannah stood at the door. "Well?" she said after Jesher had studied it for a moment. "Is it the real one?"

CHAPTER TWELVE

"I need a new face." Jesher paced the perimeter of the study, his cell phone in one hand. The light fabric of his black T-shirt tightened across his chest and shoulders as he pulled in a deep breath. He nodded into the phone before he finally came to rest on the sofa.

Jesher had set up a meeting with the contact who claimed to have the Blochet. Now he was trying to convince his half-sister to fill the role of prospective buyer. And it seemed he wasn't having a great deal of luck. He turned to Hannah and offered a brief and unconvincing smile.

Across the coffee table from him, Hannah waited in the deep armchair. His voice was calm, seductive, like he was asking a woman to dinner. But a sheen of perspiration had gathered on his face and a small vein pulsed almost imperceptibly at his temple.

"Buyers frequently accompany me. Many of them want to see the piece themselves before authorizing the purchase." He stopped and nodded while Lily spoke. "It's more common than you would think," he added after a moment.

Jesher paused again, his controlled exterior barely masking the frustration, or anger, that was gathering near his eyes. Hannah had volunteered to go with him, but Jesher had shaken her off. Too dangerous, he had said. Too many people had seen them together, he had added, though she knew it wasn't true. And then just to underscore his words of concern, he had kissed her lightly on her cheek.

"Fine," he said into the phone a moment later, "and thanks. I'll be in touch." He stood and dumped the phone into his pants pocket.

"She'll do it?"

Jesher nodded.

Hannah leaned back into the leather armchair and allowed herself to relax. It had been an unnerving few days. The Blochet that Turner had brought from Toronto was the genuine sculpture. Both she and Jesher had confirmed its authenticity. It was difficult if not impossible to copy the identifying markers: paint residue still clinging in precise places, chisel marks softened by the centuries. Even the faintest of odors that lingered in the stone proved that the Blochet now in Jesher's possession was the real *L'homme Ordinaire*. And that meant the copy on display at the Royal Victoria Museum had, at some point, been switched out for the original.

Hannah had stood at the vault door while Jesher placed the original exactly where his mother had asked. When the vault door was closed, and the locking mechanism set, he had told her he intended to buy the fake. He wanted it off the market, he had said. He wanted to study it, he had added almost as an afterthought. He needed to find out where it had come from and who had made it.

And now he was making good on his word.

Hannah knew his concerns about the fake ran deeper than just an idle curiosity. Until the Blochet's recent appearance at the Royal Victoria Museum, the sculpture had never been on public display. There was virtually no documentation on the head, save Simona's personal papers and photographs. That meant anyone capable of making such a convincing copy either must be close by or have access to the family.

Bringing the potential buyer to see the copy now for sale would legitimize the transaction. And Hannah had to agree that Lily seemed a reasonable choice. She knew enough about art to be convincing, if she needed to be so. She didn't socialize much, so there was little chance that she would be recognized. But perhaps most important, having Lily pose as a buyer would keep the transaction within the confines of the family.

The following afternoon, Jesher and Lily drove off to meet the seller of the Blochet copy. And Hannah was left to pace the huge home and hope all was well. Two hours after Jesher and Lily left, Hannah heard a car on the gravel drive. Within moments Jesher had popped the trunk and was lifting out a wooden crate. Then he handed Lily the keys to the car and brought the crate inside.

For the third time Hannah watched while a limestone sculpture was lifted from its wooden crate. She waited while Jesher brushed off the last of the packing material, and carried it into the study. Then he set it on the coffee table and seated himself directly in front of it.

Moments passed while he sat fixated in front of the head, the lifeless limestone eyes staring back at him. Then he turned the sculpture slowly around, observing each angle. At last he looked up at Hannah who stood by the door. "You'll find this interesting," was all he said.

Hannah took a seat next to him where she could take in every feature of the sculpture. The detail was precise, from the placement of the paint residue, to the incising mark that delineated the hairline. Surely its creator had an intimate knowledge of the real Blochet. A moment later, she saw what had taken Jesher's attention. Hannah ran the pad of her forefinger lightly over the edge of the deeply sculpted lip. The flaw was so slight that it could have been missed by anyone less familiar with the Blochet. But there on the lower lip was a small imperfection, a mark identical to the one on Simona's study.

"Did the seller pass this off as the original?" Hannah asked after having looked over each detail.

"He was vague." Jesher squeezed shut his eyes for a moment, then glanced around for his glasses. Once he had put them on, he shut his eyes again as if trying to clear away a blur. "He told me it was a recent, but third-hand acquisition and claimed to know little about its origins. As for its authenticity, he told me he had provenance."

"Did he?"

"In a way, yes. He had copies of some of Mother's papers. Of course copies only show someone had access to the documents." He ran his finger across the lip of the sculpture again.

"Does he know who you are?"

"I gave my name. It's best to be as transparent as possible in these kinds of transactions, I've learned."

"Except for Lily." And Hannah watched as Jesher's face darkened just a bit.

"Yes," he replied. "Except for Lily."

"So, we've got them all," Jesher said after a moment. "Three Blochets. The original, Mother's study and," he pointed to the limestone head resting on the coffee table, "this copy." He took the head and, resting it upside down on his lap, wrote his initials and the date on the bottom with a Sharpie. "It's well done," he said after a moment. "Exceptional, really. The aging of the stone, the color of the paint residue. Whoever made this copy –" but he never finished the sentence.

He didn't have to finish it. Hannah knew what he must be thinking. Someone close to the Kenyon family, someone with easy access to the Blochet, or rather Simona's copy had done the work, because the small imperfection on the lip was certainly intentional.

Jesher stood and picked up the sculpture.

"What are you going to do with it?" Hannah asked.

"I'm taking it home. I want to study it more carefully. See if it gives up any clues. The artist must have left something of himself on the head. I just need to find it."

"Is it so important to find out?" she said. "You've got the original and you've got the copy."

"I need to know," Jesher told her. Then he took the sculpture to the foyer where the packing crate stood. He pulled out a long sheet of bubble wrap and started wrapping it around the limestone.

Hannah had spread newspapers on the floor next to the crate and was dumping some of the pink plastic packing peanuts onto it when a folder of papers fell out. She picked it up and started to leaf through the pages.

"Photocopies of the provenance," Jesher said and held out his hand for the folder. "I need to study everything. Which documents were copied is as important as which ones weren't."

"Do you really think you can figure out who made the copy?" Hannah asked.

"Yes. I'm sure of it."

Something in his tone nagged at Hannah. Though he had verbally dismissed her involvement weeks before she couldn't set aside the notion that somewhere on Jesher's list of possible thieves was the name Hannah Swift. She stood silently in the foyer while he took the crate to his car.

He was beautiful and intense and possessed by great single-mindedness. And despite her best intentions, she had fallen in love with him. But she knew it had been a mistake to lose herself to a man like Jesher Kenyon.

It had been a terrible mistake.

* * *

Hannah dragged a brush through her long curly hair. The humidity had given it a mind of its own and braiding it, she decided, was the only way to tame it. She had only minutes to see that Simona had everything she needed. She gave herself a fleeting glance in the mirror, and headed down the grand staircase.

Simona had just seated herself in the garden. Next to her was Alistair. In the weeks since his arrival, Alistair Kenyon had assumed a more refined air. His hair was neatly styled, his clothes new, and his attitude more charming than ever.

This was a command performance, Simona had told Hannah. Everyone in the family had been summoned for tea at four PM.

Jesher's Land Rover was parked in the circle, though he hadn't yet made it to the garden. He was pacing in the foyer, scanning his emails. He looked up just as Hannah approached and his serious expression softened.

"Any idea why we're all here?" he asked.

Hannah shook her head.

In a single stride, Jesher closed the distance between them. He lowered his head and allowed his lips to settle against the small of her throat. "I've missed you," he whispered.

His touch made her tingle all over. She swallowed a shiver. "Simona has been keeping me busy."

"Doing?"

"This and that."

"Hmm," he said and nibbled at the lobe of her ear. "You know more than you're telling."

"The same could be said about you."

He held her back at arm's length. "Meaning?"

"There is the small matter of the extra Blochet."

"I don't know anything about it yet." Then he gathered her into his arms. "I need time to go over the statue carefully." He kissed the edges of her ear again and then whispered there, telling her how he felt and how he would make her feel.

Hannah closed her eyes for a moment and allowed herself to be set adrift in his words. But there were others around and they both needed to be in the garden. "We should go. Your mother has called a family meeting," Hannah reminded him.

"They can wait."

From the garden she could hear Simona calling to her son. Hannah eased herself away from his arms while she still could, and started for the French doors. Behind her Jesher straightened up, pushed the hem of his T-shirt into his jeans, and followed her outside.

Simona's gatherings intimidated Hannah. These were powerful people scattered casually about a hundred-year-old garden. These were people who knew fine art, who made fine art, who traded in it. Lived in it. Simona, Jesher, Alistair, even Lily had led a life of privilege. Their lifestyles formed a chasm between them and the rest of the world. Sooner or later Jesher would realize that such differences really did matter. She took a deep breath and wished Simona hadn't insisted on including her in this gathering.

""I've asked Malcolm to join us today," Simona said, "because he has been such an important part of my life and because of the history we share." Then she looked about the group. "Tea?"

Simona wouldn't be rushed. In the brief time Hannah had worked for her, Simona had held numerous family gatherings just like this one. Jesher likened it to holding court. Since his childhood, he told Hannah, his mother had summoned family members in order to share news, primarily hers. It was futile to try to avoid showing up or, for that matter, to try to interject a thought. Best to sit quietly, he had said, and mercifully hasten the conclusion. But Hannah noticed that Jesher let his phone frequently take him away and that Simona seemed to tolerate the disturbance.

Hannah took a glass of iced tea and found a place on an intricate wrought iron loveseat across a table from Simona.

"This has been quite an interesting spring, hasn't it?" Simona glanced at each face in turn and waited for acknowledgement before continuing. "I've all but completed *The Collector*. She was my first foray into cement and I have to say I enjoyed working in this new medium."

Jesher set his phone on vibrate and then stuffed it into his pocket. Lily crossed her ankles and smiled benignly. Malcolm stared at Hannah until she shifted in her seat.

"And then there's Alistair."

Hannah didn't trust herself to look directly at anyone. But next to her she could hear Jesher exhale.

"I was as surprised as you all when Alistair came home to Pinehurst," Simona went on. "But one day here he was and, well . . ." She stopped speaking and took Alistair's hand in hers. The large diamonds she wore when she wasn't working caught the light of the afternoon sun and bounced it across the garden stones.

Jesher stood.

Hannah didn't dare to breathe. Although she had seen him defy his mother, he rarely did so. He genuinely loved and respected her. Surely he wouldn't make a scene. Then a moment later she saw him dig his phone out of his jeans pocket.

"Excuse me," he said, and walked into the house.

"Let's have some pastries while we wait for Jesher. I want us all to hear this at the same time." She stood and passed a silver tray of delicacies.

The conversation wandered off to the unusually warm weather before Malcolm came to everyone's rescue with a tale of a new art acquisition. He was just about to tell how he had struck a deal with a gallery owner from New York City when Jesher returned. He slipped in next to Hannah on the love seat and offered his mother a nod.

"Before anyone else needs to take an important phone call, I'd like to finish," Simona said. "Alistair and I have reconnected."

As if on cue, Alistair reached over and patted Simona's hand.

"We were so young when we parted ways. We both realize now that it was a terrible mistake. We belong together."

Jesher took off his glasses and tossed them on the glass-topped table in front of him. Hannah glanced over and saw a fine trickle of perspiration sluice down his temple and into his hair.

"And so we have reached a decision. We want to be together and we want a fresh start. We've decided we can't have that here at Pinehurst." She stopped speaking and took a long breath. "We've decided to start our life as a couple over again in a new place." Simona paused and waited for the news to register on each person's face. Only Jesher's remained inscrutable.

"Where?" Lily finally asked.

"Fiji."

It seemed to Hannah that everyone shifted in his chair at the same time.

Simona held up one hand. "I know it seems far, but Alistair and I have talked it through and this is where we both want to be. The weather is, of course, lovely. But there are other considerations." Simona paused and took a sip of her tea. "I won't bore you all with the details, but please know that we have both given it a great deal of thought and our decision is firm. To that end," she added, "we have purchased a house with money from my holdings."

Another bead of perspiration, and then another, found its way down Jesher's cheek before he wiped them away.

For a time no one spoke. Then it seemed that everyone had questions at once. Simona held up her hand again.

"Perhaps if I can finish speaking, some of you may find answers to your questions." She placed a strategic pause while everyone quieted. "Of course there is the matter of the property," she said. "What to do?"

The quiet that now met her told her she indeed had everyone's ear.

"There have been so many necessary decisions recently. I don't know what I would have done without Alistair's help. But here it is. This is how I have decided to divide my assets."

The late afternoon air was static. Everyone assembled

was looking down at the immense quarried stones that formed the garden patio. Everyone, except Jesher. He met his mother's gaze without so much as a blink or a quiver.

"First there is Pinehurst. Besides having been my home for many years, it is architecturally important. I want to know that it's being well looked after." Simona paused and took a moment to read people's expressions. "The house and grounds are Poole," she went on. "The property needs to follow bloodlines. So clearly Pinehurst goes to you, Jesher."

Jesher reached for his glasses and put them back on.

Simona looked right at him, her eyes pinning him where he sat. "Of course I'd like you to move in. But at the same time I realize I cannot force you to do so. Still, know that I won't have it sold or rented. I'm having Jerry draw up some papers for you to sign, Jesher, to assure me that you won't."

What followed was incredible silence.

Great lengths of it.

At last Jesher stood and poured himself another glass of iced tea. He took a long gulp and set the glass back on the table. Then he jammed both hands into his pockets and walked out into the gardens.

Lily re-crossed her ankles.

Malcolm cleared his throat.

Moments later, Jesher returned. He stood at the perimeter of the gathering, his whole face dark. "Christ, Mother," he ground out.

"I won't have you swearing Jesher. Not at me or anyone else. You were raised better."

"Mother, what are you thinking?"

"This is what I want."

"Fiji? Have you lost your . . .?" He shook his head slowly.

"I'm following my heart."

"You're running off like a teenager with . . . "

"Your father," Simona said. "I'm going with your father and my husband."

"Ex-husband," Jesher said. He remained at the edge of the patio. No one but Simona and Hannah dared to look at him. He had stilled into a statue. Stone. Just like the sculptures that dotted the family gardens.

"Jesher I'm not asking permission. I'm not even entertaining your opinion. I asked everyone to come today so I could tell you all at the same time." She leaned over and patted Alistair's knee. "I don't want any misunderstandings or second-hand information traveling through the family."

Hannah watched as Jesher sucked in a long breath.

"Is that it then?" Jesher asked after a moment.

"Well, no," Simona said. "This meeting is just a first step. There are thousands of details that need attention before Alistair and I can leave. For example, there's the matter of the art." She looked over at her son. "Why don't you come back and sit next to Hannah?"

It was a small thing Simona had said, a fine acknowledgement she had made, placing her son next to her personal assistant, but Hannah would wager no one missed the finesse.

"Malcolm," Simona said and leaned forward in her chair, "I know you have always fancied the Roualt in our dining room. It's not an important work, but endlessly pretty. I'd like you to have it."

"That's very generous, Simona. I don't know what to say." He stood and rushing over to Simona planted a kiss on her cheek. "You're certain you don't want to keep all of the art in the family?"

"Malcolm, you might just as well be family. No, I've made up my mind. I'll have Jesher contact you with the details in a few days." She paused and took a sip of her tea.

"Grandfather Woolley," she continued after a moment, "was quite specific about *L'homme Ordinaire*." She stopped speaking and glanced at everyone in turn. "So of course, the Blochet goes to you, Jesher, with the understanding," she turned and looked at him straight on, "that you follow Grandfather Woolley's wishes."

"Part of the paperwork Jerry is drawing up?" Jesher said.

"Exactly," Simona returned. "Family is important and the Blochet and Pinehurst have been in this family for generations. I want assurance that they will remain so."

Jesher leaned toward Hannah until his lips were all but against her ear. "Did you know about any of this?" he whispered. "Because I could have used a heads-up."

She gave her head an almost imperceptible shake.

"To that end, I have asked Jerry to add a clause that states that *L'homme Ordinaire* will remain in this family through the ninth generation."

"Lily," Alistair said. At her name, Lily's head shot up. "Pinehurst and the Blochet were Simona's long before I met and married her. But there are certain items that she and I acquired during our marriage. Simona and I have discussed it and we both would like you to have the sterling flatware that was given to us at the time of our wedding."

"Father, that's very kind. Thank you. It's perfect," Lily said. "Just perfect."

"Well, then," Simona said and glanced about at the

group. "I believe that's all I have to say for now."

"Do you have a time frame?" Hannah asked.

"You know me, dear," Simona replied. "I've never done all that well with time frames." She turned to Alistair. "Two weeks? Three?"

Alistair nodded. "Certainly no more than that."

"Is it so important?" Simona said.

"Well, yes it is. I'll need to find a place to live," Hannah replied. "And a job."

CHAPTER THIRTEEN

"What is served, of course, is up to the madam," Jonathan said and gave a handwritten menu to Hannah. "But I think this will be to her liking."

Hannah tucked the paper into her pocket. "I'll see she gets it, and I'll let you know what she thinks before the end of the day."

A week had passed since Simona's announcement that she and Alistair were leaving for Fiji. She wanted one last gathering, a dinner this time. A happy event, she had called it, though Hannah didn't see how that was possible. Everyone would be devastated when Simona was no longer around. She brought joy to those around her, and she breathed life into everything she touched. Her sculptures as well as her home bore the proof. Simona was a force. And despite Hannah's desire to pursue a career as an art curator, she had loved working for her.

And then there was Jesher.

Hannah had hoped he would tell her to stay, that there would be work for her. And a place to live. She had hoped he would tell her he loved her, or even that he wanted more time to find out if he loved her.

But Jesher had said nothing. He had been sullen since his mother's announcement. He had barely tolerated Alistair's presence when he had returned earlier in the spring. Now Alistair and Simona were off to chase the sunset. And Jesher had been told to deal with what was left behind.

It hadn't sat well with him.

There was also the matter of the letter. Simona's imminent departure had left Hannah little time to find work, and without references she had virtually no chance of landing anything in her field. She had asked Jesher a second time for a letter of reference, hopefully one that suitably showcased her abilities and knowledge. He had said he would write it, but now, seven days later, Hannah had nothing.

Menu in hand, Hannah walked through the French doors, past the patio and down the stone path leading to Simona's studio. Pinehurst boasted several gardens, both formal and informal, all of which had been reborn under Lily's careful attention. Surrounding the patio were low boxwood hedges clipped into intricate patterns and among them stood several of Simona's earlier marble works.

Past the house, the grounds took on a less formal quality. Flowering shrubs and dozens of ferns filled in the floor of the hundred-year-old woods that stretched down to an old creek. It was a serene place and one Hannah would miss.

Hannah found Simona inside her studio, packing her art supplies carefully into a large box. "I have a menu from Jonathan," Hannah said, after knocking lightly on the door. Simona motioned her inside.

"Is it anything good?" Simona asked.

"Yes," Hannah said. "He's starting with a chilled consommé. The main course is crown roast of lamb with dressing, baby peas, steamed fingerling potatoes and a spring mix of greens for a salad. It's everything you like, except the dessert. Jonathan has suggested a layered white and dark chocolate mousse."

Simona wrinkled her nose. "He knows better." She laid

her chisels on a chamois and started rolling them carefully into a bundle. "Tell him I want Malcolm's cheesecake. Have him call Malcolm and beg if he has to. Tell him I said so."

Hannah nodded.

"And remind him that I want the salad served after the main course."

Hannah nodded again. For two years, the entire time she had worked for Simona, Hannah had reminded Jonathan that the salad was to be served following the main course. She was certain he already knew. Still, she would remind him this one last time.

"In fact," Simona said, "come here, dear. Why don't we make the whole dinner a family affair? We've already got Malcolm down for the cheesecake. Let's have Lily make the salad. She has been growing such delightful herbs this year." Simona looked at Hannah. "Think you could work with Jonathan on the fingerling potatoes?"

"Of course," Hannah said.

"And we'll leave the wine to Jesher." Simona smiled. "That way everyone is involved. It will be such fun, don't you think?"

*　*　*

Hannah slipped into a pale aqua dress. It was a skimpy affair, a froth of raw silk that fell from thin straps to skim her waist and hips. The deep neckline gave just a hint of cleavage. She took a final look at herself in the mirror, then added a pair of beige strappy heels. When she turned around Jesher was standing at the bedroom door.

"Can I come in?"

Hannah nodded and Jesher stepped into her space.

Behind him the door closed softly.

Hannah glanced at the clock on the dresser. Then she picked up her necklace, a tiny aquamarine surrounded by diamonds, and held it up to her throat. Her fingers trembled and she hoped he hadn't seen.

"Here, let me," Jesher said and took the delicate gold chain from her hands. He brushed her long hair aside, baring the nape of her neck and secured the tiny clasp. His body burned against hers. Even through his suit she could feel the heat. She wondered again, as she had for the last several days, where she would gather the courage to let go. To let him go.

"Simona is expecting me," she told him and hoped her voice sounded natural. His hands still rested on her bare shoulders. Lightly, almost mindlessly he drew tiny circles there with his forefinger. At his touch, Hannah shivered.

"Mother's going to miss you."

She turned to face him. "That's sweet. I'll miss her, too."

"You've been such a help to her."

Kind words. The words of an employer to an employee. His words were like a shrug.

Hannah let out the breath she didn't know she had been holding. "I really need to leave," she told him. "I'm expected downstairs."

For a moment Jesher just stood there, in her borrowed bedroom, not saying anything else at all. If Hannah didn't know him better, she would have thought him tongue-tied. But this was Jesher Kenyon, and so she knew better.

Hannah shifted uneasily in her four-inch heels. "Jesher?"

"I came," Jesher said after a moment, "to tell you that you're welcome to stay at Pinehurst as long as you need to."

209

"Need to?"

"There's no rush for you to leave. You can stay here in Lily's room, or move back to the cottage. It's up to you. I just wanted you to know."

A thick wave of nausea swept through Hannah. She closed her eyes briefly to gather herself. "Thanks," she said when she dared to speak. "I appreciate your generosity, but I plan to leave when Simona does." He didn't need to know more. Hannah turned away. "Simona is expecting me," she said again.

He reached into the breast pocket of his suit coat and pulled out an envelope. "This," he said, "is for you." And he placed it in her hand. "Read it over when you get a chance. If you see something you don't like, let me know and I'll change it." Then he straightened away from her. "I should have given this to you a long time ago," he said. "I just ... " He never finished the thought.

Hannah nodded. "Thank you."

"I'll see you downstairs."

And then he was gone.

Hannah set the letter on the bureau. Then she closed her eyes and listened again to his words. She was welcome to stay, he had said. She had been such a help to his mother, he had said. A deep, heavy ache filled her chest.

Hannah closed the bedroom door behind her and went downstairs to greet Simona's dinner guests.

On the first floor everyone had gathered in the study for cocktails. Simona and Alistair were seated on the sofa near the center of the room and across from them sat Lily and Malcolm. Hannah had to admit that Simona looked radiant. Tonight her hair was Simply Sweetheart red and she wore a green silk dress that dropped in folds from her

210

shoulders. Malcolm looked up briefly at Hannah and smiled before turning back to Lily who seemed pleased with his attention.

Jesher had poured himself a drink and now stood at the north end of the room, staring out the French doors. Several times he raked his hair back from his face but held himself apart from the group seated in the center of the room.

At the door Hannah watched as his shoulders rose and fell with each deep breath he took. Then in one long draught, he finished the drink he had been holding and turned around.

"Will you be joining us, dear?" Simona asked her son.

Jesher poured himself another drink, walked up behind his mother and placed a hand on her shoulder. "I'm glad you decided not to sell the house," he said to her.

His mother looked up at him and smiled. "Do you plan to move in?"

"Maybe weekends."

"I'm glad," Simona said. "Pinehurst could use you. I think it needs a bit of new life in its walls." Then she lightly clapped her hands for attention and, standing, ushered everyone into the dining room. Everyone had just been seated when Jesher's phone rang. He excused himself and wandered first into the foyer and then the study where he closed the doors.

A few minutes later he returned to the dinner party. "Sorry," he said and took a chair next to Simona. "Business."

"Well, just this once, why don't you turn your business off and put it in your pocket?" Simona said.

Without a word, Jesher switched his phone to vibrate. Moments later the consommé was served.

If Simona intended the dinner to be a happy event, it sorely missed the mark. No one, save Simona, seemed pleased with her plans to start a new life in Fiji. Simona had been a driving force in Malcolm's hunt for rare and virtually unobtainable artwork, and with her departure, he would be left without competition or impetus. Lily had spent most of her adult life managing Simona's holdings. Although she would still have her position at the bank, her responsibilities were certain to change. Jesher would be losing a friend, fellow art aficionado and most of all, a mother.

And Hannah would lose her job. And her home.

Still, those assembled chatted with Simona about her plans and tried their best to be happy for her decision.

Jonathon had just brought in the crown of lamb when Jesher stood. "Sorry, Mother. This is important. A sixteenth century Russian triptych." He pulled his phone from the breast pocket of his suit coat and walked into the study. Hannah glanced at Simona who refused to be jostled by her son's attention to business.

"The movers are coming next week," Simona said. "But Alistair and I are leaving before then. We want to be settled in our new place before the boxes arrive." She glanced at each guest in turn. "We've bought a beautiful home, but it's not overdone, wouldn't you agree, Alistair?"

Alistair nodded.

"It's actually more than a house. It's a compound. There are guest quarters and a studio for me. Of course the kitchen is in a separate building following the local custom. The entire complex is covered in a thatched roof. But it's anything but primitive. Needless to say the views are spectacular." She leaned over and gave Alistair a kiss on his cheek. "Who wouldn't be happy?"

Jesher slipped back into his seat. He took a long drink of ice water, and with his thumb pressed at the beads of perspiration that clung to his temple.

"The triptych?" Simona asked.

Jesher shook his head. "Not a done deal yet." Then he picked up his fork and took a bite of his lamb.

"We have ample room for company," Simona went on, "so I hope all of you will come for a visit. I know it's a long flight, but Fiji is just breathtaking."

Silence hung in the room. Malcolm sipped at his dinner wine. Lily cut one of the fingerling potatoes in half and then left both pieces sitting on her plate. Jesher forked up another tidbit of roasted lamb.

"You're all far too quiet. I know what you're thinking. You're thinking a woman of my age is foolish to run off to the South Seas."

No one at the table made eye contact with Simona.

"Well, seventy isn't dead. I've got a lot of living left in me and I intend to do it with Alistair. In Fiji."

She looked at her son. "You've been quiet, even for you, this evening. Aside from the unfinished business of the triptych, is anything else bothering you?"

"All is well," he told her.

But Hannah didn't think so. Despite the glaze of congeniality Jesher wore, his mother's decision to move ate at him. Hannah would just bet on it. Fine lines edged his eyes and his skin, still tanned from some midwinter trip south, looked sallow.

"If it's your business that is bothering you," Simona said and took his hand, "then you're taking this art dealing far too seriously. I believe life is meant to be more than just drudgery. It looks like you've turned your business into just that."

With the dinner and salad plates cleared, Jonathan served dessert. Malcolm had indeed brought his cheesecake, much to Simona's pleasure. "Almond," she said. "This is my favorite."

As soon as Jesher was served, he picked up his plate and excused himself.

"Oh, for heaven's sake," his mother said.

"I won't be long," he told her and slipped once again into the study, closing the doors behind him.

"Coffee or tea?" she asked when everyone had been served. Jonathan wheeled the teacart over to Simona's side. On it was a sterling silver tea service and six porcelain cups and saucers. She poured for each of her guests but Hannah could tell by the way she kept glancing toward the study that she wanted Jesher back at the table.

Hannah leaned over to Simona. "Should I get him?" she asked when he hadn't returned.

Simona waved her off. "No, let him be. He'll only leave again anyway. Better to let him finish whatever he is doing."

The conversation turned to the Picasso exhibit that was opening at the Royal Victoria Museum in two weeks. Edgar Dewald would not be in charge, Simona said. "He's taken a leave of absence. I just hope curating *Voices From The Past* wasn't too much for him." She took a sip of her tea. "He's not a young man any more."

"I don't think it was *Voices* that was too much for him," Malcolm said. "I heard he took a nasty fall."

"Oh dear. When was that?" Simona asked.

"A few weeks ago," Malcolm said.

Hannah took a bite of her cheesecake. Nasty fall would about cover the sound beating Turner said he had endured.

Half an hour later Malcolm stood. "It's been lovely, Simona, but I must go."

Lily stood as well. "Malcolm has offered to drive me home," she said, "so I'll be leaving too."

Simona walked them both to the foyer. "You'll come and visit. Promise?" Both Malcolm and Lily nodded but Hannah knew it would never happen. Malcolm was far too deeply entrenched in the movements of local society. And Lily? Well, Hannah doubted that the invitation had been sincerely delivered to her.

The goodbyes said, Simona looked about for Jesher. "Where is that son of mine? He's been busy to the point of rude, tonight."

"He's in the study," Hannah told her.

"Still?"

Hannah nodded.

"No deal can take that long. He missed dessert and coffee." She let out a long sigh and turned toward the closed study doors.

Hannah stood in the foyer. She had just days to pack. Her belongings were strewn between the cottage where she had lived for almost two years and Lily's former bedroom, where she had stayed since the attack on Turner. She would need to start right away if she hoped to be out by the time Simona and Alistair left for Fiji. It was time for her to say good night as well.

"It's a headache," Hannah heard Jesher say a moment later. She walked to the study doors and saw him stretched out on the couch his forearm covering his eyes. Simona hovered over him.

"I thought the glasses were helping."

"They were. Until tonight."

"Because if they're not doing their job," Simona went on as if he hadn't answered her, "I'd call up Dr. Chang and tell him so."

"I'm fine. The glasses are fine."

Jesher's voice was louder than usual but it wasn't strong.

Simona turned to Hannah who still stood at the doors. "He looks awful." Her face gathered into concern. "His color is off. Don't you think he looks awful?"

"I can hear you, Mother."

"Well you do. You're working too hard."

"I just need some quiet," he said in a much softer tone.

"Then I'll go upstairs," she said. "Let Jonathan know when you're leaving, so he can lock the door." She walked into the foyer, gave Hannah a kiss on the cheek and headed to her bedroom.

Hannah stood at the edge of the room unsure what she should do. It was unlike Jesher to have left the dinner guests in favor of the sofa unless he really didn't feel well. But she didn't know how to help him and maybe more importantly she didn't know if he wanted her help.

She pulled out the latches on the pocket doors and was sliding them closed when she saw Jesher press the heel of his hand between his eyes. Then he swore. It was crude and biting and some of it wasn't English.

She stopped where she stood. "Can I get you something?" she asked and walked into the study. "Tea? Sometimes tea helps."

On the table in front of Jesher was his smart phone. Next to it sat a sliver of cheesecake, barely touched. The phone started to vibrate and as it did so, it danced across the smooth surface of the table.

Jesher reached for the phone.

And Hannah couldn't help but notice his hand shaking. "Jesher," she said, "this is more than a headache."

Jesher shook his head and silenced his phone. Then he swung his feet to the floor and pulled himself into a sitting position. But his eyes remained shut.

Hannah had seen a number of Jesher's headaches, and even at their worst, they had never incapacitated him like this.

"What's wrong?" she asked.

Jesher opened his eyes but the ambient light in the study proved too much, and a moment later he shut them again. "I don't know," he said and rubbed again at his forehead.

But something was. Something was very wrong. The color had drained from his face and his skin looked sallow and damp.

"What do you want me to do?" Hannah asked.

Jesher shook his head. "Nothing. Whatever it is will pass in a few minutes." He leaned his head back against the sofa. "Go to bed, Hannah. I'm fine."

"No you aren't," she told him. "Nothing about you is fine. You're cold and you're shaking and you look terrible. That's just what I can see. Who knows what else is going on."

Jesher lay back down on the sofa and scrubbed his face with his hands. A moment later he winced and tugged at his tie until he was free of it. Then he undid the shirt button at his throat and winced again.

"Simona isn't here," Hannah said. "It's just you and me.

So why don't you tell me? And don't try to sell me that headache story because I'm not buying it." Hannah hoped her tone would mask her concern. It was hard to see someone as large and fit as Jesher unable to stay upright for more than a few moments. And harder still to see his face drawn in what must surely be pain.

Jesher lay quietly on the sofa for a few minutes before he started to shake. "I don't know," he said eventually. "I don't know what this is. It feels like the worst case of the flu I've ever had. Times ten. My skin is burning but I've got the chills."

She touched his cheek. It was cool despite the perspiration that had gathered at his temples. "What do you want me to do?"

"Maybe if I can get some sleep."

"Here? On the sofa?" It was then that she noticed his tremors had gotten much worse. She shook her head. "Jesher," she said, "you need some help. I'm calling 9-1-1." And when he didn't protest, Hannah knew she had made the right decision.

Hannah described Jesher's condition to the operator as well as she could. "I'm worried," she said when she had told him everything she knew.

"I'm dispatching EMTs right now. Stay on the line with me and stay with Mr. Kenyon."

Minutes later red lights were flashing in the circular driveway and two EMTs were rolling a gurney into the foyer of the Poole estate. Simona raced down the grand staircase, tying the sash of her robe as she ran. "What's going on?" she said.

"It's Jesher," Hannah said and put her arm around Simona.

The EMT pointed to the study. "In there?"

"Yes," Hannah said.

"What's going on? What's going on?" Simona repeated. Her face was drawn and to Hannah she looked terribly old.

"He'll be fine now Simona," Hannah told her and hoped it was the truth.

Hannah took Simona into the study where two of the EMTs were working on Jesher. One was leaning over him, taking his blood pressure. Another was kneeling beside the couch and asking all sorts of questions: name, age, occupation, address. Several times she saw Jesher close his eyes and heard the EMT repeat his name until he opened them again. To Hannah it looked like he was losing consciousness.

"Blood pressure's low," she heard someone say.

A third EMT drifted away from the group at the sofa and found Hannah. "You his wife?"

Hannah shook her head.

"Next of kin?"

"I am," Simona said. "I'm his mother. What's wrong with him?"

"Not our call. We started an IV but he is becoming less alert. We'd like to take him to Memorial so a doctor can check him out. One of you want to ride with him?"

"You go with him, dear," Simona said. Then she dropped to a chair and began to cry softly.

An EMT fished Jesher's smart phone out of his shirt pocket and handed it to Hannah. "Get whatever you need to bring with you. We'll get Mr. Kenyon into the bus."

A few minutes later Hannah was in an emergency vehicle with Jesher while the driver made his way down the highway to Memorial Hospital.

CHAPTER FOURTEEN

It was 10:15 and Hannah needed to be at the hospital. Despite his protestations, Jesher had finally agreed to stay overnight. This morning he had called to ask for a ride home. He was being discharged, he said, even though not all the test results were in.

Jesher was sitting by a small table, speaking with a doctor when Hannah arrived at his hospital room. His color had returned and the tremors in his hands had retreated. Still-damp hair clung to the back of his neck and he looked like he could use a shave. On the table sat a tray of mostly unopened food containers from the hospital kitchen.

"If you have any more symptoms, call right away," the doctor was saying. "Don't tough it out. You're lucky to have rebounded so quickly."

Jesher nodded. Then he reached for his glasses.

Hannah tapped lightly on the door and both men looked up.

"Dr. Fred McClure," the doctor said as he stood. "Are you Mrs. Kenyon?"

Hannah shook her head. "Just his ride home."

Jesher's cheeks darkened just a bit.

"Good," the doctor said. "No driving for him today. If you have any influence on him, make him take it easy. And by easy I mean he should lie down. No work." He leveled a look at Hannah. "No play, either. No nothing. His body has taken a beating over the last twelve hours." The doctor turned to Jesher. "I have some instructions here. Who gets them? You or your ride?"

No one spoke.

The doctor waited, glancing first at Jesher and then at

Hannah. "Great," he said. "The ride wins. She looks more responsible than you do, Mr. Kenyon. And I'll just bet she's more than a ride."

The doctor pressed a printed sheet into Hannah's hand. "Miss . . . uh?"

"Swift. Hannah Swift," she told him.

"Swift" He offered up a professional smile. "Bland diet. You know, clear liquids, not including gin. Or vodka. And soft things, easy to digest." He pointed to Jesher's virtually untouched breakfast tray. "Take a page. Our dietary staff here does bland better than you can imagine. It would be helpful if you did the cooking yourself. Or if he did. If he knows how. The lab hasn't pinpointed the agent yet, so the more control we have over diet, the better."

"Agent?" Hannah said.

"Generic term. We don't know what poisoned his system, but something sure did."

"Poison? You mean like food poisoning?" Hannah asked.

The doctor shook his head. "No, this was a bona fide agent, not a contaminant. We just don't know what it was, yet. But we will. The lab's still working on it."

"But we all had dinner together last night," Hannah said.

"Lamb? Peas? Salad?"

"And baby potatoes. I fixed them myself."

The doctor shrugged. "Sounds good. Better than my dinner, in fact. Except I didn't end up poisoned." Then he turned to Jesher. "You ingested something. It may have been random. In fact, it probably was. But humor me and let's go with the bland stuff, shall we?"

Jesher stood and offered his hand. "Bland it is. And

thanks."

The doctor smiled again. "Give these papers to the person at the billing desk on your way out." Then he stepped out of the room.

***

Turner was late. Hannah let out a long breath. She wasn't surprised. Turner rarely showed up on time, but he was always contrite. She had packed all of her belongings and hoped the boxes would fit in Turner's truck bed. Hannah wanted to be out of the cottage when Simona left. It would be a clean break from the entire Kenyon family.

The warm spring air felt good when Hannah stepped outside. She started down the path leading away from the cottage. Behind the patio at the main house, was Lily's herb garden. Nestled in the only area open to full sunlight, the garden was laid out like spokes of a wheel, the hub of which was Simona's marble statue of Hera. Hannah wondered if Jesher would ask Lily to stay on, if he would ask her to help with Pinehurst.

Hannah had stopped to admire the symmetry of the herb garden when she saw Lily. Her hair was held back with a bright red bandana and she wore a dark blue canvas apron. She moved quietly among the shrubs and other plantings, deadheading as she went. Hannah waved but Lily kept right on trimming.

"Good morning," Hannah said when she was near enough to be heard.

At the sound, Lily's head jerked up. A moment later she offered a brief and unconvincing smile. In one hand she held a small bucket of clippings. In the other she held a pair of nippers. She set the bucket down and stuffed the nippers into a pocket of her apron.

"The gardens are really lovely, Lily. You've done such a wonderful job with them."

"Now they'll be Jesher's to figure out," Lily said. She pulled off her latex gloves and dropped them inside out into the bucket.

"Then you won't be staying on?"

Lily shook her head. "It's not my home. None of this is mine. Didn't you hear Simona?"

Hannah was saved from responding by the sound of Turner's truck. He stopped the rusty pickup by the front door of the cottage, popped the door and hopped out. He was heading to the cottage when Hannah called to him. He waved, then leaned back against the truck and crossed his arms.

"I'd better go," Hannah said. "Turner can't spare much time this morning." She held out her hand, but Lily made no move to accept the gesture.

"Good luck," Lily said instead. Then she pulled out a new pair of gloves, picked up her bucket and headed back to complete her morning gardening chores.

"Who is that?" Turner said as soon as Hannah was within earshot.

"Jesher's half-sister," Hannah said.

Turner's face worked up a frown.

"Alistair's love child."

Turner's expression didn't change.

"Don't look like that, Turner," she said. "It happens. Alistair and Simona were young once, you know."

Turner wrinkled his nose, then levered off the side of the truck. "So, what goes in the back?" he asked and pointed to the truck bed.

An hour later they had loaded all of Hannah's belongings except a few of her clothes. She gave her brother directions to her storage unit, handed him the locker key and kissed his cheek before he had a chance to back away from her. "Thanks," she said and waved as he started back down the drive with almost everything she owned.

With the cottage all but cleaned out, Hannah went about packing the last of her clothes. She emptied the bureau drawers and was putting the contents into an orange plastic tote when her phone rang.

"Ms. Swift, I'm sorry to bother you," Dr. McClure said, "but I'm looking for Mr. Kenyon. The lab has isolated the agents that triggered his event last night."

"Dr. McClure, hi. Jesher isn't here."

There was a brief pause while Dr. McClure spoke to someone else. A moment later he was back. "Mr. Kenyon isn't answering the number we have on file and I'm not permitted to leave a voice mail. However, he did designate you as a contact on his behalf. Could you give him a message?"

Hannah said she would.

"Great. What we found is really quite interesting, medically speaking. I've never had a case of poisoning like this before. It seems that Mr. Kenyon ingested a combination of oleandroside and nerioside. Lucky that nasty little twosome didn't kill him." He paused. "Could be he didn't eat enough of whatever contained the poisons. Or, I suppose, there might not have been enough of them to do him in, given his size. All speculation on my part, you realize." He paused. "Except for the nerioside and oleandroside. I'm afraid those are quite real."

"So you just want me to give him the names of these poisons? Nerioside and the other one? Will they mean anything to him?"

"I couldn't say. But we're not talking about an allergic reaction here, like peanuts. So he may not know what they are. These agents don't occur naturally in food. They have to be put there."

Hannah sat down. "Put there?"

"Probably in tincture form. At least that's what the lab boys are saying. Tinctures are easy to add and easy to mask."

"Put there?" she said again. "On purpose?"

"Yes," Dr. McClure said, "more than likely. And, like I said, in tincture form. That's the most efficient way to get them into food. Or drink. But if I were a betting man, and I'm not, I would say food."

"So you want me to tell him he was poisoned, most likely on purpose."

"Yes, I think it prudent for him to know. Probably the police as well, but that's his call. Tell him to look up the poisons. They're more common than you would guess. Easy to find." The doctor excused himself for a moment and when he came back on the line he told her he had an emergency and needed to go.

Hannah set down her phone. She had not planned to see Jesher again. He was at Pinehurst with a staff of people to take care of him. And a mother who couldn't. But he needed to know about what the lab had reported. She glanced in the mirror, shrugged and headed toward the main house.

Hannah found Jesher on the sofa in the study, his feet propped on the coffee table. Several art catalogues were stacked on the leather cushion beside him. In front of him was a tray with a soup bowl and a small plate of crackers. Hannah knocked quietly at the door.

At the sound Jesher looked up from his laptop and motioned her in. He had worked his faced into something pleasant and benign but to Hannah it looked forced. She didn't miss the implication of his casual politeness.

Hannah tossed the smile back at him. "I have a message for you." She perched on the edge of the club chair opposite him like she knew she wouldn't be staying long. "Dr. McClure just called. He said he couldn't get through to you."

She watched his face darken as she recounted the conversation. "Dr. McClure thinks this was not an accident," she said.

"Poison?"

Hannah nodded. "Anyway," she said, "I told him I would give you the message, so mission accomplished." She stood to leave, but at the door she hesitated, and then turned back. "The cottage is almost cleaned out. I should be gone by tomorrow morning."

Jesher nodded.

And when he said nothing more, she walked out of the room.

At the front door, Hannah paused. She needed some perspective on recent events. Despite what Dr. McClure had told her, she didn't think anyone had tried to poison Jesher. And evidently Jesher didn't either. After all, he was surrounded by family at Pinehurst. If someone wished him harm it could only be beyond the circle of kin. She knew virtually nothing about how Jesher conducted his business. Or with whom. But he had acquaintance with some less than stand-up characters, at least that was the sense she got. And she also had the sense that he had, over the years, rubbed several of those acquaintances the wrong way.

But poison?

She shook her head. Nobody could hate an art dealer enough to poison him.

Except someone had.

According to Dr. McClure, Jesher had been poisoned at dinner. And that meant someone close by. That eliminated the reprobates and mobsters he knew who fancied themselves aficionados of art. And left Simona's staff and dinner guests.

"Where did you get that soup?" she fairly shouted as she turned back to the study doorway. "Did you fix it yourself like Dr. McClure told you to do?"

Jesher set down the spoon. "Lily brought it." He frowned. Nothing angry, but a frown nevertheless.

"Did you ask, or did she offer?"

"Offered." He looked at the steaming broth that filled the bowl. Then he looked at Hannah.

"Has she ever done that before, offered to cook for you, I mean?"

"I don't know. Probably not. But she was here and Mother told her I'd been sick and she probably was just trying to be helpful."

"You sure about that? The helpful part?"

Jesher gave the steaming bowl of broth a long, considering look. Then he looked up at Hannah and shook his head. "No. I know what you're thinking. But no."

"Then why did you put down the spoon?"

For a heartbeat he just stared at her. Then he reached for his laptop, opened it and started typing. "What were the toxins again?"

"Nerioside and," Hannah stopped and tried to recall the second one.

"Oleandroside," Jesher said. "Got it." He waited for the page to open, then squinted at what he saw. "Seems they do quite a job on the human body. They go to work on the digestive system and the nervous system at the same time. Lovely. Cramps, tremors, if you're lucky. That sounds about right. Death, if you're not so lucky." He continued to read silently for a moment. "The toxins are found in the Oleander bush. Twigs, berries, flowers. Every part of it is poisonous." He stopped speaking and raked back his hair. "Do we have any Oleanders on the property?"

"I don't know."

"Well, let's find out." He pulled up some pictures of the bushes and turned the computer screen to face Hannah.

"Yes," Hannah said bleakly. "They're all over. I saw Lily deadheading them this morning."

Jesher closed the computer and walked onto the patio where he found Lily by a grouping of ornamental bushes. She still had on latex gloves and she was inspecting one of the plants. At the sound of footsteps, she looked up.

"How are you feeling?" Lily asked.

"I'm fine," Jesher said and sat on one of the wrought iron benches. "Come." He patted the seat next to him. "Sit. Let's talk."

Lily stood where she was. "What's wrong?"

"Who said anything was wrong? Can't we talk?"

"Jesher, we never talk. We have spent our lives barely tolerating each other."

"Well let's give it a try anyway."

Lily frowned at him. "I have nothing to say to you."

"Are you sure?"

Lily nodded and worked her face into something quite bland and expressionless.

"Fine," Jesher said. "Then I'll do the talking. Let's start with the gloves. Gardeners don't wear latex gloves. Doctors wear latex gloves. Gardeners wear cotton or rubber or leather to protect their hands from thorns and rocks and cuts. But you, you wear latex to protect you from what?"

"I don't like dirt under my nails," she said.

"Or poison, I'd guess. Some of these plantings could make you very sick. Maybe even kill you."

Lily pulled off her gloves and stuffed them into the pocket of her apron.

"I was poisoned last night."

"I'm sorry to hear that," she said.

"The emergency room doctor chased down the toxins, oleandroside and nerioside. It seems they come from the Oleander bush."

Lily shrugged.

"Who would know something like that?"

Lily didn't answer but Hannah could see just the slightest quiver at her lower lip.

"I'm asking, Lily. Who would know such a thing?"

Lily untied her gardening apron and dropped it on the table next to Jesher. Then she walked over and stood right in front of him. She drew in a long breath and stared at him. "You don't get it do you?" she said after a moment. Her eyes were bright, her voice brittle. "For a guy who's supposed to be so smart, you really don't get it at all."

"I guess not. Suppose you tell me."

Hannah held her breath. And as she watched, Lily's face started to crumple, as if she were going to cry. But she didn't. Instead, she straightened her shoulders and looked squarely at her half-brother.

"O.K. Jesher," she said, "here it is. You are getting everything. Everything. You're getting the house, the furniture, the art. You're even getting, no you're especially getting *L'homme Ordinaire*. And why? Not because you've earned these things. Not because you deserve these things. You're getting them because you're a Poole."

Hannah shifted nervously near the door.

"Just because you're a Poole," Lily went on. "And I never will be. My birth sets me apart. My birth. How is that fair?"

Jesher took off his glasses and set them on the table. "It's not fair, Lily."

"But with you gone," she went on as if he hadn't spoken, "there is no other heir but me, Poole or otherwise. Just me. Just Lily Kenyon."

"The last heir," Jesher said. "I get it."

"You have to understand, I didn't plan to hurt anyone. That was never the plan. The plan was just to take the Blochet." She lowered herself to one of the chairs next to Jesher. "And it would never have come to this," she said, "if Edgar hadn't botched it." She stopped speaking and sucked in a shuttering breath. "He's such a wimp."

Jesher couldn't mask the surprise on his face. Hannah moved slowly onto the patio.

"What does Dewald have to do with all of this?"

But Hannah already knew.

"Edgar," Lily said, "the little fool, got cold feet. His job was to switch out the real Blochet with a copy he made. That was all he had to do." She shook her head. "I told him I would sell the real one. He didn't even have to do that. We were going to split the money. Then I wouldn't care that I wasn't a Poole."

"Edgar made the copy?" Jesher said.

"Quite the sculptor, don't you think?" Lily said. "Great attention to detail. That's what made it such a perfect plan. I supplied him with photographs and he took it from there." She stopped speaking and seemed to gather herself in a long breath.

"But the couriers brought the real Blochet," Jesher said. "Hannah watched them crate it here at Pinehurst. Then she and her brother followed them to the Vic and oversaw the setup for the exhibit."

"That's what everyone was supposed to think. It's like magic, you know," Lily said, "you see what you expect to see." She was smiling now, awash in the precision of her plan, maybe.

"So what happened to the real Blochet?" Jesher said.

"Dewald switched it out the night the couriers brought it. They were his couriers, after all. He knew what the packing crate would look like, which doors would be used, how it would be brought into the Vic. It was a great plan. Great."

"You and Dr. Dewald were quite a team, Lily," Jesher said.

"We were for a while," Lily said and smiled. "But in the end, he was, like I said, a wimp. He backed out, said he couldn't do it to his friend Simona, or some such garbage. God, what a jerk." She gave a little choking laugh. "So he put the real Blochet back in the exhibit and said he would sell the fake." She shook her head. "He said no one would notice."

"Someone always notices, Lily. There's always a tell on

a copy," Jesher said.

"I know," Lily went on. "I told him not to try to pawn off the fake. I told him he would get himself into trouble. But he just wouldn't listen to me. And look what happened to him."

Hannah shuddered. Her brother had been right. Someone had beaten Edgar Dewald.

"What do you mean?" Jesher asked.

"I told him negotiating in underground art could be dangerous. But he wouldn't listen. He's lucky he got out with just a beating."

"Do you know who did this to Dewald?" Jesher said.

Lily shrugged. "I don't have a name but it was someone who knew the *L'homme* he had was a copy. People don't like to be fooled. I told him not to try to sell it." She turned toward the French doors where Hannah was standing. "Probably the same people who worked over your brother. Although there's no way to be sure. Some of these people aren't real nice and if they think you're trying to put one over on them __. " She stopped speaking and shook her head slowly. "Well, you see what can happen."

"But my brother wasn't involved in any of this," Hannah said. "He just drove me to Toronto."

"And yet he almost died. Like I said some of these people aren't very nice."

"Lily," Jesher said. His voice was low and soothing. "You know I can't just let this pass."

"I suppose not," she said. "But you can see now why I had to poison you," she went on. "If Dewald had stuck to the plan, I'd be rich and gone and nobody would even know the Blochet had been replaced with a copy."

"Except the family."

"Of which, as Simona so frequently points out, I am not a part. So if you want to blame someone, blame Dewald, not me. Or better yet, blame your mother." She smiled up at Jesher, a glassy, brittle smile while Jesher pulled his phone from his pocket and dialed 9-1-1.

* * *

Hannah kicked off her sandals and wiggled her toes. Then she took a sip of wine from the last paper cup she had and leaned back against the sofa. She had one night left at the cottage and then she would be gone. On the floor in front of her stood her small overnight bag, the one she had packed when Jesher moved her to the main house. Everything else was now in storage. She took another sip of wine.

Jesher had accompanied Lily and the police, no doubt to tell his side of the story. Simona, Dr. Dewald, Dr. McClure and certainly Hannah herself would undoubtedly be called in for questioning at some point, but for now the mystery of the theft and the poisoning both seemed to have been solved.

And so now there was just Hannah. Her name was cleared and in a day she would be starting a completely different life. Hannah leaned back against the sofa to contemplate her next move when she saw Jesher standing at her door. She felt her heart level a single pound. "Come in," she told him.

He took a chair formally distant from her. It had been a long twenty-four hours for both of them and it showed on Jesher's face. Tiny lines worried at the edges of his lips and eyes and he still looked a bit ragged.

"Wine?" she said and then shook her head. "Sorry, I forgot. Bland diet."

Jesher leaned back in the occasional chair and crossed his ankles. Then he uncrossed them and sat up straighter in the chair. "The police may be calling you to get your version of the story," he said.

Hannah nodded.

He took in a long breath and let it out slowly. "Lily told the police everything. I guess she just wanted to come clean. Admitting the truth is cathartic even if it means things don't end well."

Hannah took a meditative sip of her wine. She watched the way he moved, the way he pushed his hair from his forehead, she listened to the gravelly sound of his voice. She wanted to cry.

"That's why I'm here, Hannah."

"Seeking catharsis?"

"Something like that." He reached forward, refilled the small paper cup with wine and took a long sip of it.

"You know my father was the logical one in our family. When I told him I wanted to be an art dealer he said I would need to learn how to be dispassionate about the art I sold if I ever hoped to have a lucrative career. Of course Mother disagreed. But my father was right." He took off his glasses and set them on the coffee table. "And over the years it's become easy for me, this dispassionate way I have about me."

Hannah wasn't sure where this was leading but she could tell that it wasn't easy for Jesher to admit.

"And sometimes I hurt people. Or worse, I don't recognize when others are hurting. Look at Lily. She was right under my nose and I didn't see her pain."

"You're not blaming yourself for what happened are you," she said, "because you had nothing to do what happened to Lily. These were all Lily's choices."

Jesher shrugged. "Maybe. But there's a takeaway for me from all of this."

"And what is that?"

"You want your own career. I get that. I do. And I don't want to stand in your way."

Hannah's stomach tightened. "That's very thoughtful of you, Jesher."

"I shouldn't have stood in your before," he went on. "I never thought you had anything to do with the theft, not really." Jesher reached across the table and took another sip of Hannah's wine. "But selling high-end art can be a tricky business. Some of these underground art dealers come up on the left side of the law."

"And what's that got to do with me?"

"I wanted you here so I could look out for you. I knew if you thought you were a suspect, you would never leave. I knew you'd want to clear your name." He took another sip of wine. "I just wanted you to be safe."

"You did a good job." Hannah told him. "Safe, I am."

Jesher stood. But he didn't say anything else.

Finally Hannah broke the silence. "It's late," she told him. "And I need to finish packing."

Then she watched Jesher Kenyon walk out of her life.

CHAPTER FIFTEEN

Hannah glanced at her phone. Her brother's smiling face stared back at her.

"Hi," Turner said. "So how's it going?"

Hannah set aside the small watercolor landscape she had been examining and put her brother on speaker. "It's going well," she told him. Late September sun poured through her office window. She squinted at her computer screen, hit save and turned away from the glaring light.

One month earlier Hannah had secured a position at Impressions, a private gallery on the east side. It didn't pay for much more than the rent, but it was a step in the direction of the career she wanted. Her first task was curating a show of local water colorists to be held in a month. Fall was a time of artistic renewal in the city and all the galleries would be hosting open houses. So the competition for securing work from the best artists was fierce. Hannah didn't have time for idle chat with Turner if she hoped to get her work done.

"What's up, Turner?" She worked to keep the sharpness out of her tone. It had been more than a month since she had heard from him. In that time he could have blown through the money she had lent him, been arrested, or taken a job abroad. With Turner she just never knew.

"I called to let you know I'm cleaning up my act. No clubbing, no drinking. Early to bed and all that." His voice cracked just a bit. "And I want to thank you for everything you did for me."

"Good to know, little brother." Hannah could only pray it was all true. "I hope you had the 'thank you' part of this conversation with Jesher. He's the one who gave you the job. And the loan."

"About that," he said.

There it was. She knew her brother, and he never called to chat. "Turner, I hope you're not going to ask for more money. Because I simply don't have it. I'm done."

"No, I'm good. But I do need a favor."

Hannah rolled her eyes. "Do tell."

"I need a new truck."

"And like I said, I'm tapped out."

"No, that's not it. I found what I wanted and applied for a loan, but the bank says I need someone to co-sign. You just started a new job, so the bank won't let you sign for me. They suggested my employer."

"Go on."

"Well that's the problem. Kenyon's not the easiest dude to talk to, in case you hadn't noticed. I tried going through his personal assistant, but she just shook her head."

Hannah glanced at her computer screen and the unfinished brochure that needed to be at the printer's by noon.

"And I was hoping maybe you could smooth the way for me, talk to him, let him know that I . . ."

"Stop right there, Turner. " Hannah's words cut across her brother's. "I have no relationship with the Kenyon family any more. You're on your own."

"So you're not still seeing Jesher? Because I was sure you two were . . . "

"I was never seeing Jesher. We worked together for a time." Well, that was the truth, the better part of it anyway. Hannah closed her eyes and when she did she could see how Jesher looked at her just before he made love to her.

She shook the image away.

"Crap," Turner said.

"Sorry."

"You were my best chance. Everybody, even Ms. McGuire says he's hard to get along with."

"He's very serious about the business, but he's not hard to get along with."

"See that's why I wanted you to talk to him. You understand him. Everyone at work just steers clear of him."

"Again, sorry. And steering clear of Jesher is something you can't do right now. If you need him to co-sign the loan, just ask him. He's a reasonable man." A knock at her open door drew her attention. "Gotta go," she said and disconnected.

Jesher Kenyon had tracked her down.

His charcoal grey suit and crisp white shirt were a testament to all that Simona had taught him about dressing for success. His hair was immaculately trimmed, his face recently shaved. But his eyes. His eyes were dark. Dangerous. And endlessly sad.

"Jesher. It's good to see you," she said because it was, and because there was nothing else to say to him, to this man who had stolen her heart.

"May I come in?"

Hannah stood and rushed to clear the only client chair of two small paintings. She propped them both against the wall and waited for Jesher Kenyon to enter her space. She waited some more while he sat. And then again while he loosened the knot of his maroon silk tie.

"You look well," he said finally.

"Thank you. You do, too."

"I'm glad you found work that suits your talents."

"It's a good job, a start for me," she said.

The niceties completed, there was an endless beat of silence.

Jesher drove his long fingers through his chocolate colored hair and Hannah watched while it fell neatly back into place like it had never been touched. And then she waited as she had so often for him to fill the conversational void.

He didn't.

"Did you come here to see the art?" she asked finally. "Because some of what I've found is very good. Maybe even great."

He shook his head. "I came here to see you."

And to Hannah it seemed like those were the hardest words he had ever said. His voice was barely above a whisper. Small creases furrowed his brow and a vein at his temple pulsed rapidly.

"Why?' she said. She hoped she didn't sound sarcastic because she hadn't meant it to be so. It was just that Jesher had said what needed saying that last night at her cottage. He had just wanted to keep her safe, he had said. Despite the proprietary overtones, the knowledge that he only had her safety in mind had stung badly. Because when she was honest with herself, she knew she hadn't gotten over Jesher Kenyon.

Not really.

Not at all.

Jesher shifted in his chair. "I made a big mistake," he said. Then he took off his glasses, just like she had seen him do hundreds of times and rubbed his eyes.

Hannah sat down. Unease crawled around her stomach. "What kind of mistake, exactly, are we talking about? Not the Blochet, I hope, because I thought that was all settled."

Jesher lifted his head and pinned her with those green eyes of his, just like he had that night in his office when she had told him the real Blochet had been replaced. "I should never have let you go," he said.

"Well, I didn't go far," she said and tried on a smile. "If there is still some unfinished business Simona left behind, I'd be happy to help out."

He looked grim, this man who had come to her office. She had seen him patch up her brother and turn his half sister over to the police and through it all he had maintained a look of strength. But she had never seen him look so vulnerable as he did right now.

"I want to try to fix my mistakes," he was saying.

Hannah started to speak but he shook her off.

"I need to finish. I've given this a lot of thought. I've been wrong before and I don't want to be wrong again. So you need to know, Hannah Swift." He stopped speaking and pulled in a long breath like maybe it was his last. "I'm in love with you. I think I have been for a very long time."

"This is what you came to tell me? Not that there's a problem with the Blochet? But that you're in love with me?"

Jesher's expression remained stark. "I'm hoping you feel the same way."

Hannah's hands started to tremble and she slipped them onto her lap.

"If you don't," he was saying, "feel the same, I'll leave you alone. I won't come around any more. That's a promise."

"In love with me?" Hannah said.

Jesher nodded. "For a long time."

Hannah let the words sink in, let them warm her like

good wine. He was in love with her, this man of few words, this man who had kept her close by his side because he wanted to protect her. This man who could have anyone he wanted, wanted her.

Silent moments passed between them and at last Jesher stood, picked up his glasses and put them back on. "OK," he said. He let out a long breath and drove his hair from his face. "I get it. I should go."

"Please don't."

Jesher stood where he was, his expression bleak. "If you need time," he said, but he never finished the thought.

"I don't need any time," she told him. "I just want to hear you say it again."

"That I love you?"

"Yes. That."

"I love you Hannah Swift. I have for a very long time." Then he walked to the side of the desk and tugged her to her feet.

"I love you, too," she said and smiled because she knew the one who loved her was truly no ordinary man.

THE END

Printed in Great Britain
by Amazon